A Hard Beginning

The McNeil Legacy, Book 1

A. K. Gentry

BRUSHY MOUNTAIN PUBLICATIONS

ISBN printed: 979-8-9950385-0-4

ISBN digital: 979-8-9950385-1-1

Library of Congress Number: 2026911135

Book Cover by Michele Welch, Old Mountain Crafts, info@oldmountainc rafts.com

CONTENTS

Note to the Reader · V

1. Chapter 1 · 1
2. Chapter 2 · 7
3. Chapter 3 · 14
4. Chapter 4 · 20
5. Chapter 5 · 27
6. Chapter 6 · 37
7. Chapter 7 · 48
8. Chapter 8 · 57
9. Chapter 9 · 63
10. Chapter 10 · 69
11. Chapter 11 · 74
12. Chapter 12 · 84
13. Chapter 13 · 91
14. Chapter 14 · 98
15. Chapter 15 · 102

16. Chapter 16 — 107

17. Chapter 17 — 114

18. Chapter 18 — 125

19. Chapter 19 — 134

20. Chapter 20 — 143

21. Chapter 21 — 149

22. Chapter 22 — 155

23. Chapter 23 — 161

24. Chapter 24 — 166

25. Chapter 25 — 178

26. Chapter 26 — 185

27. Chapter 27 — 194

28. Chapter 28 — 207

29. Chapter 29 — 217

30. Chapter 30 — 223

31. Chapter 31 — 229

32. Chapter 32 — 231

33. Chapter 33 — 233

Also by A. K. Gentry — 241

About the Author — 242

<h1 style="text-align:center">A NOTE TO THE READER</h1>

This novel takes place during a period of rapid change in both Scotland and the American colonies. In the mid-eighteenth century, many Scottish families faced limited opportunities at home due to economic pressures, shifting land practices, and the decline of the traditional clan structure. During this era, increasing numbers of Scots and Scots-Irish families emigrated to North America.

Colonial Virginia offered both opportunity and hardship. Settlers carved farms from dense forests, relied on seasonal harvests for survival, and navigated complex relationships with Native Americans. Life on the frontier demanded resilience, cooperation, and the ability to adapt to unfamiliar conditions. Scots-Irish immigrants played a significant role in shaping the backcountry, bringing with them their traditions, resourcefulness, and a strong sense of community.

The family name MacNeil reflects the Gaelic spelling used in Scotland in 1740. Upon immigrating to an English colony, the name was commonly recorded as McNeil by ship captains, census takers, and land agents. This anglicized spelling became the family's name in Virginia.

Although the McNeil family is fictional, their experiences reflect the broader realities of this period — the challenges of migration, the struggle to build a life in a demanding environment, and the quiet strength of people who endured, adapted, and forged new beginnings far from home.

CHAPTER 1

Neil MacNeil, tall and spare with thinning brown hair and clear Scottish blue eyes, stood at the window overlooking the castle's inner bailey. As Laird of the MacNeil clan, he took quiet pride in the stronghold beneath him. Vikings had ruled these rocky heights long ago, their fortified hall carved into the stone as if they meant to keep it forever. But the MacNeils had taken the island back and built their castle on top of the foundations the Norse had left behind.

Below, his three sons lingered in the bailey, talking and teasing as brothers do. John, the eldest, was already married with a son of his own, a fact that pleased Neil more than he ever admitted aloud. The family line would continue. Duncan, only a year younger, was as loyal as any vassal and twice as clever as most men at court. He always had Neil's back, and John's, when politics grew sharp. Together, John and Duncan stood shoulder to shoulder before the clan and courtiers. They were smart, strong, and when necessary, ruthless. They would carry on the family name and the clan's enterprises of trade, brewing whiskey, smuggling, and farming.

Then there was Aaron.

His youngest son had just turned sixteen and was already broader in the shoulders, taller, and stronger than his older brothers. When he was small, John and Duncan had been attentive and good-natured with him. But as Aaron grew, it became clear that he would outshine them both. That worried Neil. Jealousy could rot even the strongest family.

John and Duncan looked every inch the Highland sons, with blue eyes and reddish-brown hair that curled in the warm dampness of summer. Both stood around six feet tall. John was arrogant, loud, eager for a fight, and often too openly defiant of the British. Duncan was quieter, more thoughtful, but no less committed to the clan's prosperity.

Aaron, however, carried the mark of the old Norse blood that had mingled with the island families generations ago. He was already past six feet in height, with blond hair that waved only slightly and the same piercing blue eyes. Fastidious in his dress and bathing, Aaron drew the attention of every young woman in the castle. Athletic and disciplined, he was beginning to best his brothers when sparring, which irritated John more than he would admit.

Neil had seen the resentment growing in John, so he sent Aaron across the channel to his own brother's home to learn the art of making whiskey. Whenever Aaron returned for a visit, he brought a sample of the latest brew. Neil had to admit the lad had a talent for it.

That evening, Neil walked down the hallway toward the

stairwell that led to the great hall where the supper meal was being served. Voices drifted toward him, causing him to stop and stand in the shadows cast by a flickering torch. John and Duncan stood hidden behind a screen. John's voice carried, sharp with complaints about Aaron.

"I have a plan," John said. "We'll send him on the next trip smuggling whiskey into England. I'll let the British excise men know. Aaron will be arrested, and that will be the end to our problem."

"Why do you dislike the lad so much?" Duncan asked. "Why do you want him hurt, and what of the other men who get arrested? 'Tis not fair that their families suffer."

"Aye," John said. "That is an unfortunate consequence, but I cannot see how it can be helped, not if we want rid of Aaron."

Neil felt anger rise in his chest, but it was tempered by sorrow. He had not realized the depth of John's discontent with Aaron. It was nothing more than jealousy, but it had become dangerous.

At the evening meal, Neil and his wife sat at the center of the high table with the hall full of kinsmen. On Neil's right were John and Duncan; on his wife's left sat Aaron.

Neil leaned toward his youngest. "How are things with your uncle?"

"They are good, Father," Aaron said. "Uncle Fletcher has a fine and efficient brewing process. We are sending more barrels to England and getting a good price. He told me to say he has your share of the profits. I am to ask how you want them, in coin or supplies?"

"Tell Fletcher to do both by half," Neil said. He sat back, thinking about Aaron and what must be done. He had to protect the boy.

When the meal was finished, Neil's wife rose and withdrew from the hall. Neil motioned for Aaron to move into her seat.

"When you leave the table, go to your room. I want to talk with you in private."

"All right, Father," Aaron said, studying Neil closely. "Is anything amiss?"

"No," Neil said with a reassuring smile. "'Tis the mainland I want to discuss."

An hour later, Neil knocked on Aaron's door. Aaron opened it, and Neil stepped inside, taking the chair near a small table. Moonlight and two candles cast the only light in the room, throwing soft shadows across the walls. Neil drew a long breath, steadying himself.

"Aaron, there is a growing problem with the family. Not the clan. Our family," Neil said, and he saw confusion flicker across Aaron's face.

"You do not see it yet," Neil said, "but you are stronger, smarter, and quicker of mind than your brothers. They see it, and they are growing both jealous and wary of your successes, especially John. I fear your life may be in danger from him."

Aaron stared at Neil, stunned. "My own brother?"

"Don't look so surprised," Neil said quietly. "History is full of brother killing brother for power and control. Oh, they'll not raise a hand against you, Aaron. Do not fear that, but they will entrap you. Do not go on another smuggling run. That is an order. Tell Fletcher I forbid it."

Neil studied his son for a long moment, as if weighing a final decision. Then he reached into his coat and pulled out a belt, handing it to Aaron.

"Put this belt on."

"It's heavy," Aaron said as he took it.

Neil turned the belt over, revealing the inner lining. Two layers of gold coins were sewn between three layers of leather.

"I want you to book passage to the colonies. You can make a good life in Virginia." His gaze swept Aaron's clothes. "Wait here."

Neil left and returned with a set of clothes that would not betray Aaron as a man of wealth.

"Put these on."

Aaron obeyed. When he finished, he stood in the shirt, knee breeches, and coat of a tradesman.

"Wear your boots, but let them get dirty," Neil said. He handed Aaron a travel bag. "Here is another set of clothes and a pair of leather shoes."

He passed Aaron a pouch of coins. "This is for your passage, food, and lodging. Take food aboard the ship. Hide it and keep it near you, along with your bag and coin. Desperate people are going to the colonies. They'll think nothing of stealing from you."

Neil's expression softened. "I know your habits. I put soap and a cloth in there as well."

"Is this necessary?" Aaron asked quietly.

"Aye, son. I fear that it is. I no longer trust John with your safety. I want you to live and succeed. Take the MacNeil name to the colonies. Make us proud."

Emotion tightened Neil's throat. John was his heir. Duncan was the spare, but Aaron was his favorite, though he admitted it to no one but himself.

"Come with me," Neil said.

Neil led Aaron down the hallway to a stairwell at the

back of the castle. They descended to a wharf where two men waited beside a longboat.

"Angus and Travis will row you to the mainland," Neil said. "There is a full moon, so you'll not need a light that might betray you to anyone watching."

Neil embraced his son, and Aaron held him tightly in return.

"No talking," Neil said softly, his voice still gruff with emotion. "Sound carries over the water. Make a good life, Aaron."

He nodded to the two men, and they pushed off, the boat gliding silently into the night. Neil watched the boat disappear into the darkness. Sending Aaron off into an unknown situation was the hardest thing he had ever done. He would miss the boy terribly.

Aaron sat in the boat and watched the lights of the castle grow distant. He loved his father and his uncle, and he did not want to leave. The ache of it settled in his chest, but he understood the danger and respected Neil's determination to keep him safe.

He drew a long breath and turned toward the front of the boat. The dim lamps along the mainland shore glimmered through the cold night and grew closer with every pull of the oars. Angus and Travis rowed steadily across the narrow channel until they reached a small wharf the locals used for travel and for selling grain. Aaron stepped out and whispered his thanks. The two men pushed off and began rowing back to the island.

Aaron pulled his hat low against the cold February wind. Finding shelter in his uncle's barn, he slept a few hours. At first light, he walked to the main road and started making his way to a port.

CHAPTER 2

Norfolk, Virginia 1740

Raising his face to the sun, Aaron took a long breath of fresh, clean air. He spent every possible moment on deck unless a storm forced him below. Thankfully, there had only been one of those. Unfortunately, strong winds had been blowing hard to the east, and the storm had pushed the ship backward, costing them a full week of progress.

Today marked the beginning of the ninth week of the voyage. He counted himself fortunate. Paying extra for his passage had earned him a hammock with the crew. Most of the passengers were crammed into the hull where it was dark, filthy, and foul smelling. Some were sick. It was a good day when they did not give a body to the sea.

Adequate food for ten weeks had been loaded aboard, but now it was being rationed. Twice a day, he received one hardtack biscuit, a cup of soup, and a cup of weak beer. His stomach had never felt so hollow. He could feel himself thinning, his muscles shrinking from hunger and inactivity. The captain insisted they were making good time now that they had regained what the storm had cost them, but Aaron thought the man was either overly optimistic or lying.

"Don't look so discouraged, Mr. McNeil," the first mate said as he walked up beside him. He pointed to the horizon. "See that dark line? That's Virginia. We'll be sailing into the Chesapeake Bay and the Elizabeth River tomorrow."

Aaron flinched at the Englishman's pronunciation of his name. He liked the sound of it in his own tongue. Even the ship's captain had written it as McNeil on the passenger list. Well, he was going to an English colony. It would be better to stay quiet and accept the change.

"That's good news," Aaron said. "I had heard the crossing was harsh, but I had no idea just how harsh it could be. And yet, somehow, I think I have been lucky."

The first mate smiled. "You have been, Mr. McNeil. I have been on much longer voyages, all going to the same place."

True to the first mate's word, Aaron stood at the ship's rail the next day and watched the landscape along the Elizabeth River pass by. Wharves bustled with barrels of grain being loaded for market. Fields were being plowed. Forests and swamps stretched beyond the banks. Everything fascinated him.

The crew tied the ship to the wharf moorings. He was finally in Virginia. Passengers poured up from below. The crew placed a makeshift bridge from the ship to the pier. Aaron stood back and let the first wave of passengers rush past. The stench rolling out from the hull was overpowering. No wonder they were desperate to escape it.

"What's next for you?" Aaron asked the first mate, who stood beside him.

"The crew cleans the hull," the man said. "Then we pack it with tobacco, cotton, molasses, timber, corn. Whatever the colonists want to sell. There will be plenty of furs, too."

He extended his hand. "My name is Edward Montgomery. It's been nice traveling with you, Mr. McNeil."

Aaron shook the man's hand. "Please, I think it's time you called me Aaron."

Edward studied him. "How old are you, Aaron?"

"Sixteen, sir," Aaron replied.

"Ah, a good age to start the life of a man. Come into Norfolk with me. I have a friend who runs a tavern. I imagine he could use some help for a few days until you get your bearings and decide what comes next."

Aaron followed Edward Montgomery off the ship, along the wharf and up a cobblestone street. He took in the sights, smells, and activity of the young city in the New World.

"Keep your eyes open," Edward said. "Most folks here are good people, but there is still the desperation of lost hopes and the struggle to succeed in an entirely new way of life. That makes thieves. Norfolk is small and not nearly as bad as New York, Boston, or Philadelphia." He turned down a street lined with shops and stepped into the Running Hare Tavern.

A man behind the counter looked up. "Edward! You're back. How was the trip, and how are things in England?"

Edward grinned. "The trip was one of the better ones, and England is the same. James, I want you to meet a young friend of mine, Aaron McNeil. Aaron, this is James

Montgomery, my uncle."

"Pleased to meet you, Mr. Montgomery," Aaron said.

James tilted his head. "Is that a Scottish accent I'm hearing?"

Aaron stood tall. "Aye. I'm Scottish, and proud to be."

James laughed and clapped Aaron on the shoulder. "Good for you. Stand tall and be proud of who you are."

He eyed Aaron. "Now, would you be one of those Scots with a talent for making whiskey? Scotland is known for its fine spirits."

Aaron smiled. "Aye. I have the knowledge."

James's eyes brightened. He reached under the cabinet and brought out a small cup of whiskey.

"Taste this. Tell me what she needs."

Aaron took a sip. He blinked and coughed. "Well, she could be a bit smoother."

James roared with laughter. "I agree. How would you do that?"

"I would mix barley with your grain, add a wee bit of honey and yeast, and let it ferment longer before putting it in the still," Aaron said. "I think the water is making a difference, too. I'm used to the cold stream water of northern Scotland. This is different."

James nodded thoughtfully. "Aaron, I will give you a place to sleep, food, and a shilling a month if you will work here in the tavern and make whiskey and ale."

Aaron grinned. "I would be grateful for the job and place to stay. I'll make you famous in Virginia for your brew."

James chuckled. "I'll settle for Norfolk famous. Come to the back."

He led Aaron behind the counter and into the kitchen.

A young woman was cutting pieces of meat and placing them in the large pot over the fire.

"Mary, I brought you some help. This is Aaron McNeil."

James looked at the young man. "Aaron, this is my daughter, Mary Montgomery. She may be bonnie and easy on the eyes, but be careful, my boy, she has a tongue that can cut you to ribbons."

Mary turned, smiling. "It's nice to meet you, Aaron. Don't listen to my father; he will make fun of you in a moment."

Aaron smiled back. She looked to be about his age, petite with dark hair and hazel eyes. Her skin was a smooth olive complexion that probably never burned in the sun the way his did.

"It is nice to meet you, Mary," Aaron said. "I will be working here, so tell me what you want me to do."

Mary laughed. "Goodness, imagine that. Me bossing a man like you around."

Aaron glanced down. She barely reached his chin.

"Come this way, Aaron," James said.

He took Aaron out the back to another building. The floor had been dug a few inches into the ground, making it firm and hard packed. One side of the room was cool and housed potatoes, turnips, apples, pears, and carrots. The other side was warm with a small fireplace. Two copper pots sat in front of it, each holding a corn mash that was struggling to ferment. A still sat over another small open fire near the pots.

"All right, Aaron, what do we do with this?" James asked.

Aaron sniffed the mash. "It's working, but slowly." He took a ladle off a hook on the wall and carefully tasted the mixture.

He grimaced. "I think we could fertilize the garden with that."

Aaron looked around and found bins of wheat, rye, and barley. He put some wheat and barley in the mortar and pestle and ground it coarsely. He poured that into the mix along with a little molasses that sat near the apples.

"Let's see what this does overnight."

"That's it?" James asked. Edward was watching and trying not to laugh.

"Yes, sir. You've got your fermented mash, but I'm just trying to soften it out a little to a more mellow taste." Aaron added another log to the fire in the hearth. "The heat needs to be a little higher to warm the pots."

"Huh," James said and walked over to two large vats of fermenting wheat. "What about my ale?"

Aaron tasted it and coughed.

"You have the right idea, but I think you've used too much yeast." He poured more water on the mixture and added a handful of wheat kernels.

James watched him, then said, "Come on, I'll show you where you can sleep."

He led Aaron back into the pub and up a set of narrow stairs. A trapdoor in the ceiling opened to a floored attic with a mattress lying on the boards.

"You can stay here when you can. If it's too hot or too cold, you can sleep in the kitchen or the root cellar. Just take your straw mattress with you and put it back in the morning. Mary should have a spare blanket somewhere. She keeps a few sheep out back for the wool, and we slaughter one now and then for mutton. There are two cows in the barn for milk, butter, and cheese. Mary could use help with the milking."

James eyed him. "You have milked a cow, haven't you?"

Aaron blushed. "No, sir. I've never milked a cow. But I can learn."

James looked at Aaron then at Edward and back to Aaron.

"Why am I getting the impression that even though you're dressed like one of us, you're really a nob?"

Edward laughed. "I think he's somewhere in the middle, James. Am I right, Aaron?"

Aaron shrugged. "Where I lived and grew up does not matter. 'Tis where I am now that does. I can learn anything I set my mind to."

"Educated, too," James said. "Good. The customers can't cheat you if they're handing their money to you."

Aaron left his bag in the attic and followed the men downstairs.

"James," Edward said, "Aaron and I could use some breakfast. All we've eaten for two weeks are hardtack biscuits soaked in weak beer. We did get fresh water during one storm, which helped."

James turned to his daughter. "Mary, these boys need a breakfast, then you can put Aaron to work."

Mary set two small meals before them.

Edward smiled. "Start small, Aaron. Too much food today will make you sick. Your stomach needs to readjust."

Aaron nodded and ate slowly.

By nightfall, Aaron was exhausted. After weeks of inactivity and poor food on the ship, the work felt good, but he tired easily. He climbed into the attic and fell asleep almost instantly.

Chapter 3

Norfolk, Virginia 1740

Edward Montgomery stayed at the Running Hare each night and worked aboard the ship during the day. A few days later, he came into the tavern in the early afternoon.

"James, we are sailing on the evening tide," he said. "Thank you for a clean bed and good food." He put some money on the counter and lowered his voice. "This is your share of the profits. The cargo didn't stay in the warehouse for more than two days. The demand for goods is growing." He paused. "Keep an eye on Aaron, will you? He is young and green. He needs a guide to help him adjust to this new world. He has no idea how harsh it can be."

James nodded. "I'll do that. I like the boy, and he's already improved my drink. Word is spreading."

"Let him work on the farm," Edward said. "Teach him that, too. He needs all the skills before he sets out on his own. He's a good lad. He'll make a good man, one you're lucky to call a friend."

Edward found Aaron in the backyard chopping wood. "Aaron," he called.

Aaron looked up and smiled. "Edward! You're back early."

Edward smiled. "We're sailing on the evening tide. Would you like me to take a letter back to England to make its way to Scotland?"

Aaron grinned. "Maybe next time. I've got to earn enough money to buy paper and ink."

Edward nodded in understanding. "Just on the chance I can pass a word along, who should I inform that you made it safely to Virginia?"

"I doubt that your paths will cross," Aaron said, "but if you should meet Laird Neil MacNeil, you can tell him I am safe and learning a new life."

"A Laird's son?" Edward raised his brows. "You must have quite a story if your father sent you to the unknown wilds of the colonies. I'd like to hear it sometime. I'll see you on my return voyage."

Aaron shook Edward's hand. "I am glad that we've become friends. I pray your voyages continue to be swift and safe."

"Thank you," Edward said. "Work hard and learn. This is a hard life if you are not prepared, but I have confidence that you will thrive here, Aaron."

"Thank you, sir," Aaron said, and he watched his new friend walk toward the wharf.

Life in Norfolk settled into a rhythm of farm work, distilling, and helping in the tavern. The days were long, but Aaron found they suited him.

"That's right," James yelled. "Keep her straight, now."

He watched Aaron struggle to keep the oxen pulling the plow in a straight line. He grinned. The corn might be in wavy lines, but it would still be planted.

The Running Hare Tavern faced the street, but James owned the fifty acres extending behind the building. He grew the food he served in the tavern and the grain for his ale and whiskey. Extra grain came from the local farmers eager to sell their surplus. Beyond the tavern, new houses were rising along the growing streets of Norfolk.

The wide dining room of the pub occupied the front half of the building. The kitchen sat at one end of the back half. Two bedrooms opened into the kitchen where Mary worked. Upstairs were three rooms for rent, and at the end of the narrow hallway was the trapdoor to the attic.

Aaron finished the plowing and brought in a load of wood for the kitchen fireplace.

"Let me see your hands," Mary said when Aaron dropped the wood.

He held them up.

Mary smiled. "They're getting tougher. No more blisters."

Aaron smiled. "No. Just calluses. I was used to work, but almost three months of inactivity on the ship made them soft."

"Work?" Mary teased. "Definitely not farm work. But you're learning fast. That's good."

Aaron grinned. "No, not farm work."

"What did you do?" Mary asked.

"I worked for my uncle," he said. "I ground wheat, barley, and rye coarsely for the brewing. I chopped wood and kept the fermenting room warm and steamy. And I drove the wagon to the town to buy sugar, honey, molasses, and grain. My uncle hired farm workers to do the plowing and planting. I never learned, but I'm happy to learn now.

Growing food is a useful skill, wouldn't you say?"

Mary laughed. "Yes. I would say so." She studied him for a moment. "Is it true? Did you grow up in a large castle? Father described what a castle looked like."

A shadow crossed Aaron's face.

"Aye, I was born in a castle. My father is Neil MacNeil, Laird of the MacNeil clan. I am the third son. My oldest brother, John, is the heir and future Laird, and he already has a son himself. My next brother, Duncan, is only a year younger and entirely devoted to John. They're forming a strong partnership that will lead and protect the clan. That's a good thing. I'm not complaining."

He paused. "I was born eight years after Duncan. I do not look like them, act like them, or think like them. They are all Scotland. I look and act like the Vikings that were there before my clan ran them out. Vikings married the Scottish women. Some of that blood runs in my family. I am more like my uncle and grandmother than my father. That's why he sent me to his brother, Fletcher, to learn brewing."

His voice softened. "Father overheard my brothers talk of letting me walk into a British trap to get me away from the clan. The other two will lead the clan, but I am my father's favorite. So he sent me to Virginia to save my life. My Scottish name is MacNeil, but the English changed it to McNeil."

"So, you were born and educated as a gentleman," Mary said softly.

"Aye," Aaron said.

Mary's expression shifted, distant and wistful.

"What?" Aaron asked.

In a small voice, she said, "I wish I could read and write."

Aaron blinked in surprise. He knew not everyone was educated, but he had assumed that Edward Montgomery's family would be.

He smiled gently. "Let's make a bargain. If you sew and repair clothes for me, I will teach you to read and write. And if you help me learn the ways of Virginia, I will teach you numbers."

"You would teach me?" Mary whispered. "A girl?"

Aaron shrugged. "Why not? Girls can learn, too."

Mary's face lit. "We have a bargain. When do we start?"

"Let's go to the garden," Aaron said.

"Garden?" she echoed.

Aaron motioned for Mary to follow him. On a smooth patch of dirt, he drew the letter A with his finger and explained its sound. They laughed at the difference in the sounds between his Scottish A and her Virginian A. Once he used a word as an example, she understood.

Aaron gave her four letters: A, B, C, and T. When she could write them, he spelled "cat" in the dirt.

"C-a-t spells the word for cat," he said.

Mary stared. "That's the word for cat? I can read the word cat?"

"Aye," he said, pleased with her reaction.

Tears glistened in her eyes.

"I can read a word," she whispered. She looked up at Aaron. "Thank you. Show me some more."

"Practice those," Aaron said with a laugh. "We need to get back to work. There are a lot more letters and words to learn. Be patient and learn them well."

Spring eased into summer. Aaron watched the seeds he had helped plant grow tall and fruitful. Mary and James taught him the life cycle of each plant and how to tell when the produce was ripe. Aaron taught Mary the alphabet, spelling, and reading.

Distilling whiskey and brewing ale were the same as in Scotland. Aaron began to experiment with the fermented mash for ale. Chopped apples in the mix gave the ale a fruity flavor. Chopped potatoes made it drier, less sweet. By midsummer, he had barrels of different ales in the storage room. Local customers began favoring certain types, and James's business grew. He increased Aaron's wages.

By late summer, Aaron had grown another two inches. His muscles broadened and strengthened from the hard labor. Mary struggled to keep up with the sewing needed to keep him decently clothed.

Overall, Aaron was pleased with the way his new life was progressing.

CHAPTER 4

Norfolk, Virginia 1740

In the middle of September, Aaron was bringing a load of firewood into the kitchen when Edward Montgomery walked back into the tavern.

"Edward!" James exclaimed. "I'm glad to see you back, safe and sound. How was the crossing?"

"The sea is getting very choppy, James," Edward said. "Bands of clouds are forming. You'd best harvest what you can and get it inside. I fear a bad storm is coming."

James trusted Edward's instincts about the weather. He closed the front door, and the four of them headed to the fields behind the tavern.

"My word!" Edward exclaimed as he crossed the yard. "Aaron, you're still a growing lad! I hardly recognized you."

Aaron smiled. "Mary wishes I would stop. She's the one who keeps my clothes sewn and decent."

Mary shot Edward a wry look, grimaced, and nodded.

They worked quickly, gathering all the ripe vegetables and storing them away. James cut the barley with the scythe while Mary, Edward, and Aaron bundled it and carried it to the storage room, placing it near the bin of oats already harvested. By late afternoon, the sky had darkened, and the wind came in sharp gusts. The corn was nearly ready, so they walked through the rows and picked everything dry enough to store.

Light bands of rain began passing through Norfolk when they finally returned to the kitchen. Mary brought in several buckets of water from the well and filled every pitcher they owned.

Edward and James sat resting while Mary and Aaron went back out to secure the sheep and chickens and milk the cows. They returned with milk and eggs. Finally, they sank heavily in their chairs.

"I think that's everything," Mary said.

"Thank you, Edward," James said. "You've saved the business. We managed to get most of the food inside. Now, if the roof stays on, we'll be fine."

The rain grew heavier, arriving in sheets and blowing sideways. Aaron noticed water trickling down the inside of the fireplace.

"The wind is blowing the rain under the shelter you have over your chimney," he said. "If it weren't there, your fire would be out by now."

James smiled. "That's happened before. That's why I built the cover. Let's hope the wind doesn't blow it off."

Edward turned to Aaron. "When we got to London, *The Bonnie Lass* was moored near us. Your father was in London on business for his clan and the MacDonalds, and I was able to meet him." He smiled. "Your father is a fine man, Aaron. He was pleased to hear you had safely arrived in Virginia and found work. He warned me that your brothers still do not know where you are. He gave me this to pass along." He handed Aaron a small box.

"My mother was a MacDonald," Aaron said. "Father has one of the best ships in Scotland and frequently goes to London for both clans."

Aaron ran his hand across the top of the box, then opened it. A letter lay on top. Beneath it were several coins and a ring with the McNeil coat of arms. Aaron lifted the ring reverently and slipped it onto his finger. After a long moment, he removed it and placed it back in the box.

Clearing his throat, Aaron said, "Excuse me, please. I think I will go into the dining room to read my letter."

He left the kitchen and took a seat by a front window where the light was still good enough to read by. Picking up the letter, he broke the seal and began to read.

Dear Aaron, it is a blessed day to hear you are safe and well in Virginia. I keep you in my prayers daily for safety and success. You cannot know how relieved I am that you are safely away from here. Your brothers are bewildered by your absence. John is more than a little concerned that you will return strong and overthrow him. Also, politics here are becoming dangerous. There is a movement to rekindle the Jacobites' effort to restore James Stuart to the throne. If it fails, any Scotsman involved will be imprisoned or deported. Make your way in your new home, Aaron. Send me word and make me proud. With affection, Neil MacNeil.

Aaron blinked back tears. He placed the letter back in the box and looked at the coins. Mary would be pleased that he could buy a proper set of clothes from a tailor.

Aaron put the box in his bag, then removed his mattress and belongings from the attic to a second-floor room. He did not want the letter or the ring anywhere near a leaking roof.

Mary looked up when he walked back into the kitchen. "Did you have good news?"

"Aye," Aaron said. "Father is glad I am well, but he says it is not safe to return to Scotland. My older brother is paranoid instead of relieved that I am gone. And politics are worsening. There's talk of restoring James to the throne, and I imagine Scots trust neither the English nor each other now. But I do not think I want to return anyway. I am building a new life here, and it can be more than anything I would have had in Scotland."

A sudden crash echoed from across the road. All four jumped. Aaron ran to the window.

"A tree has crashed onto one of the buildings," he said. "I'm going over to make sure everyone is safe."

"Bring them here," James said.

Aaron ran across the road and into the damaged building. Moments later, he was helping a woman walk toward the tavern. A man followed, pressing a towel to his bleeding head.

"Is anyone else inside, John?" James asked.

"No. It was just us." John Simmons turned to Aaron. "Thank you. That was a fright. And thank you, James, for giving us shelter."

Mary took the towel from the man and examined his wound.

"You'll need a stitch or two," she said. She left the room and returned with whiskey and her sewing kit.

"Drink," she said. "This will hurt."

John drank, and Mary stitched the wound closed. After dipping a corner of the towel in a small amount of whiskey, she washed the wound and cleaned the blood from his hair.

"Thank you, Mary," John said.

Mary turned to Abigail. "Are you unhurt?"

"Yes," she answered. "I was nowhere near the tree when it fell."

"And the baby?"

Abigail smiled, resting a hand on her belly. "Still warm and snug."

The wind got stronger, and more crashes sounded along the street. Aaron rushed out each time to check on their neighbors. Before long, a dozen people gathered in the tavern's dining room, waiting out the storm. The sun set, and the room grew dim. Firelight and a few candles kept the darkness at bay. After midnight, the wind finally eased.

At sunrise, rain fell, but the wind had died to a light breeze. People lay scattered across the dining room floor where they had tried to sleep. Aaron stood and looked out the window. Trees were down, and water ran through the street like a river.

Mary started breakfast in the kitchen. Abigail and another woman helped her prepare hot bread and butter, oat porridge, and tea or coffee.

By mid-morning, the rain slackened to a drizzle, and sunshine broke through the southern sky. The men went outside to assess the damage and begin cleaning debris. Edward left to check on his ship.

After lunch, Edward returned, fetched Aaron, and took

him to the wharf. An ox and wagon waited. The sailors used ropes and pulleys to unload the cargo. Edward and Aaron joined in. When the first wagon was full, Edward replaced it with another one. He drove the loaded wagon away, returned with an empty one, and the process continued until the ship was empty.

Edward spoke with the captain. The damaged ship was moored to what was left of the wharf, and repairs would start the next day. After paying the crew and sending them for food, he arranged for them to sleep aboard the ship. Later, he took the ship's cook into Norfolk to buy provisions. Many farmers were selling whatever they could salvage from their gardens, grateful for any coin.

That evening, Mary, James, Aaron, and Edward served a full dining room. Several ships had been damaged, and their crews sought food and drink. The Running Hare remained busy until nearly midnight. When James finally closed and locked the door, the four collapsed into chairs at the kitchen table. Too tired to speak, they cleaned up and went to bed.

Mary rose at dawn to bake bread. Aaron milked the cows and brought in the milk and eggs.

"Fewer eggs this morning," he said. "I guess chickens don't like storms."

"Not storms like that," Mary agreed.

Edward entered the kitchen. "That bread smells wonderful, Mary. Is it done?"

Mary pulled a loaf from the brick oven James had built in the hearth. She sliced it, and they spread butter and blueberry jam over the warm pieces. Mary added cheese and poured four cups of tea.

"Mary, this was delicious," Edward said. "Thank you."

"This is our usual breakfast," Aaron said, "but it tastes different this morning. Better."

"That's because we're grateful," James said. "We came through the storm with so little damage." He looked at Edward. "Thanks to you, we didn't lose food like so many others. It may be a lean winter."

Edward nodded. "The ship needs quite a few repairs. I'll pay the crew to do that. When they're completed, I'll keep her here for a few months. I don't want to cross the Atlantic in the winter. It's no fun to survive a storm then freeze to death in January."

"What about the warehouse?" James asked.

"It was undamaged," Edward said. "I have the cargo inside and part of the crew guarding it, but I don't expect it to stay very long. Merchants need to replace inventory, and everyone has had some sort of storm damage. We'll be making a profit for sure." He paused. "James, the wharf is damaged. If we repair it, we basically own it. If we keep it in good repair and supply equipment for unloading cargo, then every captain needing a berth pays us for the privilege. I can hire someone to run the waterfront. What do you think?"

James grinned, already seeing the coin it would generate. "Sounds good. Let's do it."

CHAPTER 5

Norfolk, Virginia 1740

A week after the storm passed, most of the debris had been cleared, and repairs were underway on buildings up and down the street. The crews of stranded and damaged ships were more than happy to work for a small wage.

Edward came into the pub for dinner. He motioned James over, and they sat at a table and talked.

"Most of the cargo is gone," Edward said. "I believe this is the fastest that we have ever sold a shipload of goods. Shopkeepers in Norfolk and Williamsburg bought most of it. I'm saving some of the iron tools, cloth, tea, coffee, and dishes to make a run to the Caribbean for sugar and rum." He handed James a pouch of money. "Your share. How do you feel about buying one of the abandoned ships at the wharf? We can keep two ships sailing, carrying cargo and passengers."

"I like that idea," James said. "But I think it would be better to hire an agent to sail with the ships and get the goods to and from London while you stay in Virginia and handle the business from here. I can expand the tavern with more dining room space and another room or two upstairs. You can buy cargo to ship to England. The money we make here can easily purchase cargo. And Aaron is a master at brewing. If I could get decanters, I'd sell it by the bottle."

"I think you're right," Edward said. "There was a reluctant sailor on board this trip. Educated, looking to find his way here. I wondered if he was a much younger son in a gentry household. I'll talk with him about the position."

James laughed. "Like us?"

Edward laughed with him. "But the fortune is ours. I cannot imagine living that boring, stuffy life again. There is nothing boring about the New World."

"You handle the negotiations and hire your agent," James said. "I'll run the tavern and inn."

"I saw sails up the river. Another ship is coming in this afternoon. I'll buy what cargo I can and mark up the price to the shopkeepers or take it with me to the Caribbean." Edward stood, grabbed one of Mary's apple tarts, and headed toward the door. "I need to get to the docks."

That evening Aaron had finished milking the cows and was walking back to the kitchen with the buckets of milk. A flicker of movement in the dimming light caught his eye. He set the buckets inside the door and stepped into the shadows of the building. Two small figures darted along the barn and slipped into the storage shed.

Aaron moved quietly to the shed and opened the door. The two shadows bolted for the exit, but he caught them, one under each arm, and carried them toward the back of the tavern.

The children screamed, "Let me go. We ain't stealing

nothin'. Let us go."

Aaron realized they were speaking Gaelic. He answered in the same tongue. "I'm not going to hurt you."

The children froze. Aaron set them down but kept a hand on their shoulders.

"If you're no' stealing, why were ye sneaking into my root cellar?" Aaron asked.

The little girl burst into tears. The boy, slightly older, clenched his jaw, trying hard not to cry.

"Are ye hungry?" Aaron asked.

Both nodded, tears streaking down their cheeks.

"Promise not to run away, and I'll get ye some food."

"We promise," they said.

Aaron held their hands and led them into the kitchen. He helped the girl into a chair and motioned for the boy to sit.

"Can ye speak English?" Aaron asked.

"Aye," the children answered.

"Good," Aaron said. "You must speak only English in Virginia. What are your names?"

"I'm Michael Brown, and she's Emmy Brown," the boy said.

"Where are your parents?"

Emmy's face crumpled, fresh tears running down her cheeks.

"Da died on the boat," Michael said.

Mary set pieces of buttered bread in front of the children. They each grabbed a piece and started to devour it.

"Slowly," Aaron said. "You'll make yourselves sick if you eat too fast. I know; I was on one of those boats meself."

The children slowed their chewing.

"Where is your ma?" Aaron asked.

Emmy started to cry again. "We were supposed to get food. Ma needs food."

"Where is she?" Aaron asked firmly.

"Out there," Emmy whispered, pointing to the back of the property.

Aaron looked at Michael. "Show me where your ma is."

Michael hesitated until Aaron said, "I cannot help your ma if I don't know where she is."

Michael nodded and led him outside.

"Why were you coming to Virginia?" Aaron asked as they walked.

"There was no more work for Da back home," Michael said.

"How old are you?"

"I'm nine. Emmy is seven."

As they walked toward a small patch of woods, Aaron said, "I don't have any family here either. My family is in Scotland. Where is yours?"

"Scotland," Michael said.

They stepped into the trees. A few feet from the edge, a woman lay on the ground, half hidden by a bush.

"Ma," Michael said softly. "I've got help."

The woman opened her eyes. When she saw Michael and Aaron, something like relief passed across her face.

Aaron bent and gently lifted the woman. She was skin and bones, barely weighing more than a child. Cradling her against his chest, he carried her back to the tavern.

Edward, James, and Mary looked up as Aaron carried the woman inside.

"Mary, do you have some broth we could feed the woman?" he asked, already heading up the stairs. He laid her carefully in the bed of a vacant room.

Mary soon arrived with a cup of warm broth. She held it to the woman's lips.

"Drink this slowly," she said gently.

The woman sipped, then whispered, "Thank you. My children?"

"Michael and Emmy are fine, but they are worried about you." Mary glanced at the door and motioned for the children to enter.

Michael and Emmy hurried to the bedside. Emmy was still crying. "Ma, please get better."

"I will," the woman whispered, managing a faint smile. Relief softened her face, though exhaustion still pulled at her features. "Do what these nice people say and don't be in the way." Her eyes closed, and her grip on the children loosened as sleep overtook her.

Mary led the children back to the kitchen, the men following behind. She gave the children another small piece of bread, then joined the men at the table.

Edward spoke quietly. "I imagine she gave her children most of her ration of food. That's how it looks to me."

"We can't just leave them to starve," Aaron said.

"No. We'll get them well," James said. He looked at Mary. "You could use some help, and the woman will need a way to provide for the children."

They all glanced at the children who had finished eating and were watching them with wide, uncertain eyes.

Mary went to Emmy and crouched down to her level. "Emmy, you can sleep in my room until your mother gets well." Mary pointed to her door.

Aaron said, "Michael, we'll make you a mattress, and you can sleep where I do, which is anywhere that is comfortable."

James shook his head. "Aaron, take the other spare room. Put your mattress on the floor for Michael."

"Yes, sir," Aaron said.

Mary saw Emmy yawn. She took the child by the hand to the outhouse, then settled her in the room to sleep. Aaron did the same for Michael.

When Emmy was asleep, Mary carried another cup of broth upstairs. She woke the woman gently and coaxed her to drink more of the protein-rich liquid.

By the next morning, the woman was more alert. Mary handed her another cup of broth.

"I'm Mary Montgomery. What's your name?"

"Megan Brown," the woman answered. "Thank you for helping my children and me."

"You're welcome," Mary said. "We've helped newcomers before, but you are the sickest we have seen. You gave your children most of your food, didn't you?"

"Aye," Megan's voice trembled. "Our ship blew off course. The captain rationed the food. Paul, my husband, and I shared one ration. We gave the children their rations and part of ours. Paul caught the fever and died." A tear slid from the corner of her eye and ran down into her hair.

"I'm sorry," Mary said softly. "He sacrificed himself so your children could reach land healthy. He was a noble man."

"Aye, he was," Megan whispered.

"Do you need help to the outhouse?" Mary asked.

"Aye, please."

Mary helped her down the stairs and outside. When

Megan was finished, Mary guided her back to the kitchen and eased her into a chair.

Aaron entered carrying two buckets of milk; Michael and Emmy trailed behind him. Michael ran to his mother and hugged her. Emmy followed, wrapping her arms around Megan's waist.

Megan kissed their heads. "Are you being helpful?" They nodded eagerly.

Aaron walked over to where Megan was sitting. "I'm Aaron. Michael helped with the milking, and Emmy collected the eggs."

James and Edward stepped into the kitchen.

"Mary," James said. "I need two bowls of porridge, bread, butter, and hot tea."

Mary prepared the order and placed it on a wooden tray. James carried it to the dining room.

"This is a tavern?" Mary asked.

"Yes," Edward said. "My uncle and I own the tavern and a shipping business."

Megan said, "I can cook and wait on customers if you need help. I need a job."

Edward smiled. "You get well, Megan. We'll discuss a job when you're able."

"I can work now." Megan tried to stand, but her legs wobbled.

Edward steadied her and eased her back into the chair. "Let's give you another day or two to strengthen up. Michael and Emmy have already proven they are willing to work."

The back door opened. Megan watched as Aaron brought in a load of wood. Michael followed him with a smaller load, and Emmy came behind them carrying two tiny pieces of wood, which she proudly placed on the stack.

Edward grinned and looked at Megan. "She's a bonnie lass, Megan. Sweet as she can be."

Megan smiled. "Aye. She is all that."

Mary entered the kitchen with a few potatoes.

"Hand me those, a knife and a bowl of water," Megan said. "I'll peel them for you."

Mary smiled and passed her the items along with another cup of broth.

"If you can keep that broth down, I'll give you some bread later in the day," Mary said.

She chopped a portion of meat and dropped it into the large pot. She poured water over it, added a pinch of salt, and swung the pot over the fire using the hinged iron hook.

Megan watched. "That's clever. Your hook moves."

"Father had the blacksmith make it," Mary said. "The fire burns hotter in the back. I can move the pot to get the heat I need."

Megan peeled the potatoes while Mary chopped a small yellow vegetable.

"What's that?" Megan asked.

"Squash. It flavors the stew and thickens the broth."

When the water simmered around the meat, Mary added a handful of green stems with white bulbs and several dried pods.

"What are those?" Megan asked.

"Wild onion." Mary held up a pod. "And these are leather britches. Dried beans. The hull softens and releases the beans into the stew."

Megan shook her head. "I have a lot to learn about this

new world."

Mary smiled. "Take your time, and be open to new ideas." She reached into a sack and added two handfuls of dried corn.

"And that?" Megan asked.

"Maize. Corn. We plant the three sisters together. Corn, squash, and beans. They grow in harmony and give us the bounty of their contentment."

"Where did you learn that?" Megan asked.

"My mother," Mary said. "She was Nottoway."

"What's Nottoway?" Megan asked.

"Her people. They were here before the white men came. She met Father when she and her brother came to trade furs. Father says he took one look at her and fell in love."

"That's right," James said, entering the kitchen. "Morning Rain was the sweetest, most beautiful woman I had ever met. Red Wolf, her brother, didn't want her to marry a white man, but he didn't forbid it."

Megan looked at James. "You say was. Is she not here?"

James's expression softened with grief. "She died giving birth to our son who also died. Mary was only seven, about Emmy's age. That was a hard time. There were no children here for Mary to play with. Morning Rain had been taking Mary to the village. Red Wolf continued that, giving Mary a chance to learn the Nottoway ways and play with the children."

James handed Mary two carrots. "Mary, you know I like my carrots."

Mary smiled. She scraped the dirt from them, washed them, cut them, and set them aside to add later.

"What's a carrot?" Megan asked.

James grinned. "I traveled a lot before coming to Virginia. I tasted carrots in Persia. I liked them and brought seeds. We grow a few here. They need different soil and a warmer climate, but they do all right."

"Mary," James said, "when we've eaten the noon meal, I'll put out a sign for your stew. We'll make some money today."

James turned to Megan. "No one in the area can beat Mary's stew for taste."

Mary laughed. "The three sisters are happy in the stew, along with the other things we grow."

When the meat was tender, she added potatoes and carrots. She sliced bread and set out a bowl of butter. When the stew was ready, Aaron, the Montgomerys, and the Browns had their first meal together.

"We need a bigger table," James said, laughing.

Mary noticed with satisfaction that Megan ate a small portion. After the meal, James placed a sign in the window advertising Mary's stew. Before long, single men with a few coins in their pockets lined up for a bowl of stew, a slice of bread, and a tankard of ale. James sold every bit within an hour.

CHAPTER 6

Norfolk, Virginia 1740

Late October draped the land in a canopy of flame-colored leaves, and the north wind threaded through the branches with the promise of colder days ahead. Megan had regained most of the weight she had lost on the voyage, and the Brown family had settled into the Montgomery family as naturally as Aaron once had.

Mary, Megan, and Emmy spent the morning collecting persimmons. Mary taught them how to judge the ripe ones and how to use them in recipes.

James, Aaron, and Michael were in the forest cutting wood. The cooler weather demanded more fuel to keep the mash fermenting, and the brewing shed now consumed wood at a remarkable pace. Earlier in the month, James and Aaron had dug a separate root cellar for the apples, potatoes, wild onions, butternut squash, turnips, and sweet potatoes, freeing the entire building for brewing.

Megan still marveled at the variety of foods in Virginia. Mary reminded her that not every family enjoyed such variety. James had tasted tomatoes, carrots, and okra during his travels abroad. He liked them enough to bring seeds to Virginia.

Mary and Megan had returned to the kitchen and were shaping dough for more bread when the back door opened. Megan startled at the sight of a copper-skinned man with long dark hair, dressed in buckskin leggings, skirt and shirt. Mary's face lit with recognition.

"Red Wolf," she said warmly. "I am glad to see you."

The man smiled. "Are you well, Dancing Rain?"

"Yes. Do you have furs?"

"I do. Where is James?" he asked.

"In the forest cutting wood. Much has changed since you were here last. Come in, sit, and eat."

Mary placed a tankard of water and a bowl of stew before him. Red Wolf sat without acknowledging Megan. Mary gestured toward her.

"Red Wolf, this is Megan Brown. She and her children, Michael and Emmy, have become part of the family. Her husband died on the voyage from Scotland."

Red Wolf finally looked at Megan, gave a brief nod, and turned back to his stew.

After a moment, he asked, "Who is the tall yellow-haired man?"

Mary smiled. "That is Aaron. Edward brought him from one of the ships. He was just a boy then. He has grown up fast in Virginia."

Red Wolf's eyes sharpened as he looked at Mary.

Mary corrected herself. "He has grown up fast in Cheroenhaka."

She turned to Megan. "That is the Nottoway name for this land. They still claim it as theirs, even though the

English have built towns here."

The back door opened. James stepped inside and placed wood by the hearth.

"Red Wolf!" he said, grinning. "I thought that was your horse and furs out back. Welcome."

Red Wolf rose, and the two men grasped each other's arms at the elbow before James clapped him on the shoulder.

"Sit, finish your meal," James said. "Mary has grown skilled at the hearth, has she not?"

Red Wolf smiled at Mary. "Dancing Rain is skilled at many things."

"When you're done," James said, "we'll take your furs to Edward. He has opened a trading post and general store. He will give you a good price. You can barter for supplies or money, whichever you prefer."

After eating, Red Wolf carried his fur pelts to Edward. When he returned, his horse was laden with blankets, food, and tools. He found Mary in the kitchen.

"Dancing Rain, I would talk with you."

Mary handed Megan the ladle and followed him outside. Between the tavern and brewing shed, he stopped.

"You have not been to the village in a long while," he said. "Your grandparents grow old. They wish to see you."

Mary's expression softened. "I wish to see them, too. I will tell Father."

She turned toward the kitchen then paused. "Red Wolf, I would ask that Aaron McNeil be allowed to come, too. He has asked to learn the ways of this land, and I believe you could teach him. In return, he has taught me to read and write the white man's language and how to use their numbers. He can teach you, too."

Red Wolf considered this. "He would teach us this written language?"

"Yes," Mary said.

"Bring him," Red Wolf decided. "Such knowledge will be valuable."

Aaron had stepped into the yard while they spoke. He understood none of the Nottoway words but sensed the seriousness of the exchange. He walked into the barn to give them privacy.

Mary went into the tavern to speak with James. She explained her grandparents' request and her desire to go.

James nodded. "You should go."

"Father," she said, "I want Aaron to go, too. I promised to teach him the ways of this land if he taught me reading, writing, and arithmetic. He has done that, and I need to uphold my end of the bargain. Red Wolf has agreed."

"Then you'd better ask him," James said with a faint smile.

Mary found Aaron in the barn, brushing down one of the horses.

"Aaron," she said, "I am going with Red Wolf to visit my grandparents. I asked him to teach you the skills a man needs in this country, and he agreed, if you will teach him to read as you have taught me. He will teach you to hunt, trap, track, and survive in the wilderness."

Aaron paused, absorbing the weight of the offer. "Will James allow it?"

"He said to ask you if you wished to go."

"I do," Aaron said without hesitation.

He and Mary went into the tavern to speak with James.

That evening, Red Wolf joined the Montgomerys and Browns at the supper table. After eating, Mary slipped away to pack a change of clothes.

Later, Aaron handed his small wooden box to Edward.

"Would you keep this safe for me?"

"I will," Edward said.

"There's money in there," Aaron added with a grin. "Use it to make a profit and me a rich man."

Edward chuckled. "I'll try. Bring back some furs, and I will make you richer still."

At first light the next morning, Mary and Aaron set out with Red Wolf. Aaron carried a large knife and the flint-lock rifle he'd purchased from Edward with his earnings. As they walked, Mary began teaching Aaron the Not-toway language, simple words at first then phrases. That evening, Aaron gave Red Wolf his first reading lesson, the same one Mary started with. Red Wolf marveled that he could already read one English word.

The next day Red Wolf began teaching Aaron to read the forest, the differences between animal tracks, how to tell fresh prints from old, how to follow a trail without losing it. On the third day, Red Wolf shot a deer. He showed Aaron how to drain the blood properly. Then they tied the deer's legs to the trunk of a small felled tree. Carrying the ends of the tree on their shoulders, the two men walked into the village.

The people in the village rushed toward them, call-ing out greetings to Red Wolf and Mary in rapid Not-toway. Many stared openly at Aaron. An elderly man and woman approached Mary, cupping her face in their hands and speaking softly. Aaron heard his name among their words.

Mary suddenly laughed. She turned to him, her eyes bright.

"Grandfather says you look like a big pale bear. That is your name now, Pale Bear."

Aaron grinned. "I have a Nottoway name? That's..." He shook his head. "I'm honored."

Mary translated, and her grandparents nodded, smiling warmly before pulling Mary toward their lodge.

Red Wolf clapped Aaron on the shoulder. "Come on, Pale Bear. We must skin the deer."

Aaron eyed him. The man was trying not to laugh.

"You think Pale Bear is funny? Why?"

Red Wolf's mouth twitched. "It's what Mary did not tell you."

Aaron raised an eyebrow. "What did she not tell me?"

"They said you look like a big ugly pale bear," Red Wolf said, breaking into laughter.

Aaron stared at him then laughed. "They did not!"

Red Wolf laughed harder.

Aaron shook his head. "You're funning me."

Red Wolf taught Aaron to skin the deer and save the hide. The women divided the meat. Red Wolf showed him how to scrape the fur and preserve the hide for buckskin. Before dark, Aaron had Red Wolf practice writing the letters and simple words he'd learned, then added more.

Each day, Red Wolf took Aaron hunting. Each day, they brought back a deer or turkeys. Aaron grew more skilled at skinning and preparing the hides. He set a simple trap in the woods and caught rabbits, giving the meat to the women and saving the fur.

One afternoon, Aaron noticed several young men talking with Red Wolf and glancing his way. He caught enough of their words to suspect a challenge was coming.

Red Wolf approached Aaron. "The young men want a contest. They want you to enter."

Aaron narrowed his eyes. "Is that so they can laugh at how poorly the ugly pale bear performs?"

Red Wolf shrugged, amused. "Perhaps. But they compete often. This time they are inviting you."

Aaron smiled. "All right. What do I do?"

Red Wolf handed Aaron a bow and arrow and pointed to a target. "Hit the center. Closest wins. You shoot last."

Aaron watched each man take his turn. Their form reminded him of hunting in Scotland. When his turn came, he hit the target cleanly, earning a respectable third place.

Next came knife throwing. From twenty feet away, Aaron barely hit the target. The others cheered.

The final contest was hatchet throwing. Aaron considered the weight and balance of the hatchet, tossing it lightly from hand to hand. Scots were no strangers to axe contests. Finally, it was his turn. He sighted the distance and threw the hatchet. He hit the center of the target.

For a moment, the men stared in stunned silence. Then they erupted into cheers, slapping him on the back.

Red Wolf nodded. "You did well. You have earned some respect. Now, let's go check your traps."

Aaron found a rabbit caught in each of his traps. He carried four rabbits back to the village, carefully skinned them, and handed the meat to the women. Mary was working with them, her hands moving with practiced ease. Aaron stepped closer.

"Mary, are you enjoying your visit with your grandparents?"

Mary smiled, though sadness softened the edges of it. "Yes, but it is bittersweet. This is likely the last time I will see them. They may not survive the winter. The storm ruined much of the food they had stored for the frozen months when nothing grows."

"Can I help?" Aaron asked.

"You already are," Mary said. "Every deer and rabbit you bring back has been eaten or dried into jerky for winter stew. They salvaged some of the corn and leather britches, but they lost a great deal."

"Do they need more meat?" Aaron asked.

"Yes," Mary said.

"Then I'd better go hunting," he said and walked away. He did not see the soft, grateful smile Mary gave him.

Red Wolf and Aaron moved silently through the forest, following a faint track of game. Red Wolf lifted a hand, signaling Aaron to be still and quiet. A musky scent drifted on the wind. Aaron glanced at Red Wolf, who gave a small, knowing smile and crept forward.

They were downwind from a massive black bear. The men raised their rifles and fired in unison. The bear collapsed instantly.

"That thing is huge!" Aaron exclaimed. "How do we get something that big back to the village?"

"We get help," Red Wolf said. "It is not far. Take the trail back to the village. Tell Mary you need men and women to come for the meat. She will tell them."

Aaron ran back to the village, and soon a large number of Nottoway men and women arrived with baskets and containers. The bear was skinned, cut, and carried away piece by piece until nothing remained but the imprint of its body on the leaves.

Aaron began searching the forest every day. He found a black walnut tree and filled his shirt and hat with nuts. Every few days he trapped rabbits or shot a deer. Once he found a persimmon tree still heavy with fruit. His single purpose was to provide food for the village.

One afternoon, Red Wolf found Aaron at a creek.

"What are you doing?" he asked.

"Laundry," Aaron said. "My shirt is filthy, and it stinks." He wrung it out and laid it over a bush. "That will have to do. Maybe it will smell better."

Red Wolf chuckled. "Come with me. And bring your shirt."

Aaron followed Red Wolf back to the village. Mary met him with a bright smile.

"Stand there," she said.

Women emerged from their lodges carrying buckskin garments. Mary explained.

"You have helped the village, and everyone is grateful. The women have been busy." She grinned. "You are a very big man, Pale Bear."

She held up the garments. "They have made you leggings, a loincloth with a skirt, a long shirt, moccasins and a coat. And they still did not use all the hides you provided."

Aaron touched the soft buckskin. "These are beautiful, Mary. Tell them I am grateful. Tell them thank you. And ask them how I'm supposed to put the leggings and loincloth on!"

The village erupted in laughter.

Red Wolf clapped him on the back. "Come into the lodge. I can show you."

When Aaron emerged, dressed in everything but the coat. He turned in a slow circle and said, "Thank you," in Nottoway, earning cheers from the village.

One morning Aaron went outside the lodge to find frost glittering everywhere. He went back inside and pulled on the buckskin shirt. It was warm enough that he didn't need the coat. Virginia was a lot warmer than northern Scotland. He had struggled with the heat and humidity, and the cooler air felt like a blessing.

Red Wolf joined him. "Let's check your traps."

Aaron wore moccasins now. Red Wolf taught him how to walk silently, how to place his feet so the forest barely noticed him. Aaron learned quickly. They approached a doe and her fawn without being detected until Red Wolf purposefully snapped a twig to send them running.

On the walk back to the village, Red Wolf said, "You have learned much about the forest. Practice will make you better. Now, you must learn to fight."

"Fight?" Aaron asked.

"Yes. Peace does not last forever, Pale Bear. My people resent the white man taking their land. The animals grow scarce from so much hunting. The Nottoway resent it, but the Mohawk, Huron, Shawnee and Cherokee are angry. They will fight for what is theirs. The English want the French lands. The French want the English gone. The Huron have allied with the French. War will come someday. You must be ready."

"What do I need to learn?" Aaron asked.

Red Wolf asked Aaron to explain how the French and English fought. Then he described how the Nottoway and other tribes fight, from behind cover. They strike from the trees, firing when the enemy reloads, then blending back in the forest.

Back in the village, Red Wolf taught him hand-to-hand combat, how to fight without a gun. Aaron was clumsy at first, but he learned quickly. Within a few days, he could hold his own in the contests the Nottoway men enjoyed.

He found he liked wrestling and sparring well enough, but it was the game of stickball he liked best. Only later did he learn that the French called it lacrosse.

CHAPTER 7

Virginia Tidewater Region 1740

One evening in the middle of November, Mary approached Aaron where he stood near the lodge fires.

"It is time for me to return to Norfolk," she said. "Are you coming, or do you wish to stay here?"

"I'll come with you," Aaron said. "Is Red Wolf going, too?"

"Yes. He plans to take me to Norfolk then spend the winter at a hunting camp he keeps in the mountains." Her voice softened. "In the spring he will trade furs with Edward for supplies for the village. It will not be a long hunt for him. He will return in early spring. My grandparents are old and frail. When grandfather dies, Red Wolf will become the tribal leader, and he will not be as free to hunt and trade."

"That is sad in so many ways," Aaron said quietly. "I'm sorry. I know you understand the cycle of life but losing the ones you love is still difficult."

Mary smiled and touched his arm lightly, almost without thinking. "You are kind, Aaron. Thank you." She turned and walked back to her grandparents' lodge.

Aaron watched her go, the firelight catching the swing of her braid. His fingers drifted to the place on his arm where her hand had rested. She had never touched him before. So why did his chest feel tight, as if something inside had shifted?

Inside the lodge, Mary paused just inside the doorway. Her face felt warm. Why had she touched his arm? Why did her stomach flutter as though she'd swallowed a handful of butterflies?

The next morning, Mary said goodbye to her grandparents. Aaron thanked them for their hospitality. He felt the weight of the moment in Mary's lingering hug with her grandmother and Red Wolf's steadying hand on his father's shoulder.

Outside, Aaron watched Red Wolf say goodbye to his wife and children. There was gravity in the man's posture, a quiet acceptance of duty and the narrowing freedom ahead of him. Then the three of them stepped back on the trail to Norfolk.

Aaron had several rabbit furs tied to Red Wolf's horse. Mary glanced at them.

"What are you going to do with your rabbit furs?"

"I thought about trading them with Edward," Aaron said. "Do you have a better use for them?"

Mary nodded. "You should line your moccasins with them for the winter. Without the lining, your feet could freeze."

Aaron nodded. "You're right. I'll do that. Do you need any of them? If you do, you may have them."

Mary smiled. "Thank you, but let's get you fitted for

winter first. I'll show you how to make mittens with the furs. And you can sew a lining for the inside of your coat for the really cold days."

That night on the trail, under a sky sharp with stars, Mary showed Aaron how to use dry sinew to stitch the furs into mittens and moccasin linings. The fire crackled, throwing light across their hands as they worked. In return, Aaron gave Mary and Red Wolf more lessons in reading and numbers, their voices low and steady in the quiet woods.

Two days later, at noon, the three of them stepped into the warm, bustling kitchen of the tavern. The smell of bread, smoke, and roasting meat washed over Aaron. It was so different from the trail.

Megan looked up and broke into a wide smile. "Mary, Aaron, Red Wolf. It's so good to see you return."

James heard the commotion and strode in. He swept Mary into a long, fierce hug.

"I missed ya, girl. I always do."

"I missed you, too, Father," Mary said, her voice muffled against his shoulder.

James turned to Aaron. "Aaron! I almost didn't recognize you! You've gotten even bigger, and you're wearing buckskins! Did you outgrow your clothes?"

Mary and Aaron laughed, and Red Wolf's mouth curved into a slight smile.

"I learned a lot, James," Aaron said.

Mary added, "Aaron hunted and brought so much food into the village that the women made him a set of clothes, moccasins, and a coat."

Aaron gave a sheepish grin. "The buckskins will last

longer than my other clothes. They're worn thin."

James chuckled. "I bet Mary's glad you can make your own clothes now."

Aaron looked at Mary, amused. "You were behind this, weren't you?"

"Maybe," Mary said, giving him a quick wink.

Aaron felt a flutter of butterflies in his stomach when Mary winked at him. He shook his head, telling himself the flutter in his stomach was only hunger.

Aaron and Red Wolf had brought several turkeys to the tavern. Mary and Megan quickly had them roasting on a spit over the fire, the rich smell filling the kitchen.

That night, everyone celebrated the trio's return to the tavern with roasted turkey, butternut squash and wild greens. Megan had made small tea cakes for dessert.

"Where did you get the sugar?" Aaron asked James.

"Edward had a ship take cargo to the Caribbean. He brought back sugar and rum," James said.

Aaron looked at Edward. "Thanks. These are good."

Later, when the tavern was quiet, Aaron lay down in a bed for the first time in weeks. The mattress felt almost too soft after sleeping on furs on the ground. It was comfortable but strangely unfamiliar. He realized he was learning to live between two very different worlds.

The next morning Red Wolf approached Aaron. "I'm going hunting and trapping. You are welcome to come with me. See what's in the west. Bring back some furs."

Aaron smiled. "I would like that."

"You need to buy a horse," Red Wolf said. "We walk. The horses carry supplies."

Aaron spent the day getting the supplies Red Wolf told

him he would need. He lined his moccasins with extra fur and fashioned a sturdier hat from felt and fur. That night, Aaron had trouble falling asleep. He was excited for this new adventure.

By morning, everything was loaded on the horses, and the two friends were preparing to leave. Mary stepped into the yard with a small bundle in her hands. She offered it to Aaron.

"Bread and tea cakes," she said with a smile. "Be safe, and come back with lots of furs."

As she spoke, she placed her hand on his arm. Aaron tried to focus on her words, but the warmth of her touch seemed to burn straight through his buckskin shirt to his skin.

He followed Red Wolf through the back of James's property. When he glanced over his shoulder, Mary was smiling and waving. He waved back. A faint, unexpected sadness tugged at him. Why was he sorry to be leaving? He shook the feeling off and lengthened his stride to keep pace with Red Wolf.

They walked to the wharf and paid for the ferry to take them to the west side of the river. The main road traveled west, and they followed it until just after noon when Red Wolf turned onto a narrow path disappearing into the forest. Most settlers would never have noticed the trail, but Aaron had learned well; he could follow it easily, even without Red Wolf leading.

That evening they camped by a bend in a small river. Aaron prepared bread and dried jerky while Red Wolf set two traps in the river. At first light they checked them; both held beavers. The animals were skinned, and Aaron flash fried the meat in thin strips on the iron skillet he carried on his horse. They ate what they needed and wrapped the rest for the coming days.

Autumn's daylight was shrinking. The men walked before dawn and well after sunset. After several days, they found themselves on a small, well-used road. When they rounded a curve, Aaron got his first glimpse of the mountains rising in the distance. He stopped in his tracks. He was used to the jagged peaks of Skye, but these were different. They were higher, broader, and stretched across the horizon in a way that made his chest tighten. He had never seen mountains like these. The sheer height and breadth of them stole his breath.

While they traveled the settlers' roads, the two men talked. When they traveled the forest paths, they walked quietly. Red Wolf continued to teach Aaron wilderness survival, tracking, sheltering, and reading the land. At night they softened hides and preserved furs by firelight, and Aaron continued teaching Red Wolf to read and write.

By late November, Aaron and Red Wolf were starting to climb steeper trails into the mountains. Whenever their meat supply dwindled, they trapped another animal, saved the fur, and cooked the meat. In early December, a storm dropped several inches of white, powdery snow. Red Wolf showed Aaron how to stay warm and sheltered in such weather.

After a month of travel, Aaron realized he had never been this high in the mountains. He'd never lived in the Scottish Highlands, but he had visited and didn't remember them standing this tall.

They were traveling along the top ridge of a mountain

when Red Wolf stopped. He smiled. "We're here."

Aaron looked around. All he saw was the mountainside and, several yards away, a sheer drop on the other side of the trail.

"Where are we?"

Red Wolf smiled. He took a stick, pushed aside a curtain of vines, and revealed the mouth of a cave. Holding the vines back, he motioned for Aaron to lead the horses inside.

"Stop," Red Wolf said. "Look at the ground. What do you see?"

"Various prints. Small animals and one large one. Oh!" Aaron looked at Red Wolf. "A very large set of prints."

"Always check the prints before going far into a cave," Red Wolf said.

The men got their rifles and left the horses at the cave entrance. Moving slowly toward the back, Aaron heard the faint rush of water. The passage opened into a large cavern behind a small waterfall.

Red Wolf studied the prints on the ground. "It goes that way," he said, pointing to a tunnel that sloped upward. Red Wolf moved behind a rock wall of the cave and lit a fire; the flames began throwing long shadows across the dirt floor.

"Let's check the rest of the cave," he said.

Torch in hand, Red Wolf led the way. Aaron stayed alert; he recognized the familiar musky odor of bear.

"It's near," Red Wolf murmured.

A soft movement echoed through the tunnel. Red Wolf touched a depression on the ground.

"It was sleeping here. The ground is still warm."

They followed the sound up the tunnel. The passage

opened into another chamber, and they saw the bear climbing out through a narrow opening in the hillside. From the mouth of the opening, they watched it run into the forest.

"Let's go get the horses," Red Wolf said.

They brought the horses into the cavern behind the waterfall, unloaded them, and gave them water and oats. On a ledge behind the rock wall sat a wooden chest. Red Wolf opened it and placed their food inside.

"This keeps the food for us and not for other animals."

He loaded several traps in the panniers, and they led the horses back through the vines to the trail. Red Wolf mounted onto his horse.

"Now we ride."

They rode up the mountain. On the summit, a small river wound through the forest and a meadow. They set beaver traps in the water.

On the way back, Red Wolf said, "Stop." He pointed to the ground. "That's a big hole. It opens to another room in the cave. Mark it in your mind. You don't want your horse to fall in and break a leg."

Aaron studied the trees and rocks until he was sure he could find the spot again.

Several days passed in the same routine. Check traps, retrieve the animal, reset traps. Skin the animal, dry the meat, prepare the hide and fur.

One day, Red Wolf said, "Enough trapping here. It is unwise to take all the animals. They will have babies, and there will be more here next year."

A storm swept through, leaving several inches of snow on the ground and keeping them in the cave for a day. When the weather cleared, the men followed deer tracks.

They shot two deer, smoked the meat, and prepared the hides for buckskins.

Every time they climbed the mountain to hunt, fish, or trap, Aaron looked around. He liked the place. The top of the range felt more like rolling hills than mountains. The longer he stayed, the more he thought of the area as a future homestead.

CHAPTER 8

Appalachian Mountains, Virginia 1741

In late January, Red Wolf said, "Pack some food and the sacks we brought. Time for a different hunt."

"What are we hunting?" Aaron asked.

"Salt."

Aaron blinked. "Salt? In the mountains?" He only knew the coastal method, boiling seawater. "Where?"

"West," Red Wolf said. "We climb the ridge and cross the valley. The salt is on the west side."

Aaron studied him. "If we are looking for salt, who else is looking for salt?"

"Seneca, Iroquois, Ottawa, Creek, Shawnee, Cherokee," Red Wolf said. "Everyone needs salt. It is neutral ground, unless two tribes at war meet."

"Of course," Aaron muttered. "Are there any tribes at war?"

Red Wolf laughed. "Always!"

They readied the horses and started west. The climb up the ridge was brutal. The wind tore through Aaron's fur-lined coat as if he wore nothing at all. Only when they descended did the air soften enough for him to feel his fingers and toes again.

At the base of the mountain, Red Wolf said, "We camp here tonight. Tomorrow, we cross the valley, gather the salt, and return."

They built a shelter and took turns keeping watch. At first gray light, they ate dried venison and continued their journey.

They were approaching a sharp curve in the trail when Aaron heard faint voices. Red Wolf signaled to stop. They dismounted and crept through the trees.

Two white men rode ahead of them, talking loudly, oblivious to the world around them. They were also searching for salt.

Red Wolf's jaw tightened. The men's leisurely pace slowed everyone's progress, and their clumsy, rhythmic clatter was an open invitation to every scout within five miles. Still, the four men eventually crossed the valley, and the trail opened to a broad clearing. Years of digging had pitted the ground into a wasteland of craters and churned earth. Underfoot, a crust of salt crunched like broken bone. The air smelled faintly of animals that frequented the lick.

The two white men walked straight to the middle of the clearing and began digging. Red Wolf led Aaron along the tree line to a small peninsula of untouched salt about a hundred yards away. They worked quickly and quietly, filling their panniers with sacks of salt.

Aaron and Red Wolf were easing back into the forest when a scream split the clearing, followed by coarse laughter. Aaron turned first, heading to the main clearing. He saw a young girl, barely a teenager in worn buckskins, struggling in the grip of the two men. He handed his reins to Red Wolf.

"Cover me," he whispered, then stepped out of the trees, keeping his hands visible and empty. He walked toward the men, who eyed him warily.

Aaron thickened his Scottish accent. "Good afternoon. Am I in the right place to find salt? I had been told this was the spot."

The man holding the girl sneered. "You best leave, boy."

Aaron smiled pleasantly. "Why? I just got here, and I need salt. Where are you from?"

"None of your business," the other man snapped. "You heard Jep, leave!"

"Ah, Jep," Aaron said lightly. "Nice ta meet ye. I'm John. John MacNeil."

Jep's eyes narrowed. "I don't care who you are. Get on with ya. Leave."

Without looking at the girl, Aaron said in Iroquois, "Run to the woods behind me."

Jep stiffened. "What did you say to the girl? Who are you?"

"I'm John. I told her to run," Aaron said.

Jep shoved the girl away, drew his knife and lunged toward Aaron. Aaron sidestepped, driving a kick to the man's back. Jep landed face first in the dirt. The second man raised his rifle. Before he could fire, Aaron grabbed the barrel of the gun while his hatchet flashed across the man's throat in a single, instinctive stroke. The man collapsed.

Jep charged again, his knife blade extended. Aaron dropped the gun and swung the hatchet hard, aiming to disarm the man. The blade struck Jep's forearm, severing the bone. The knife dropped. Jep stared at the wound in disbelief, blood pouring from his arm. He staggered, tried to lift the knife with his other hand, then faltered as the shock overtook him. He collapsed to his knees, then to his side. The blood slowed as his heart failed.

Silence fell.

Aaron stared at the bodies, horror rising in his throat. He had meant only to distract them long enough for the girl to escape. He had not imagined this. He never thought to kill them. Tears filled his eyes, his stomach heaved, and he stumbled behind a boulder to vomit.

A hand touched his shoulder. Aaron spun around, but it was only Red Wolf, steady and calm with concern in his eyes. He had been watching from the trees, rifle shouldered and ready to intervene if necessary.

"You are unhurt, Pale Bear," Red Wolf said. "You learned well. You fought well. If you had not, you would be dead. Take pride. You survived."

Aaron wiped his mouth, shaken. "I've never killed any-one. We were taught it is a sin. I don't know why it never crossed my mind that they would try to kill me." He gave a weak, bitter smile. "I have a lot to learn about human nature. I thought because they were white and I am white, we could talk. I've never been so wrong."

"What of the girl?" Aaron asked, looking around.

"She ran to her people," Red Wolf said. "They are camped north of here. They had been gathering salt, and no others had been around. She thought it was safe to fill one more sack. She learned today that it was not and that she should not come alone."

They gathered the dead men's weapons, money, hors-es, and saddlebags. When the men's sacks were full of salt, Aaron and Red Wolf started back across the valley.

Aaron rode in silence, replaying every moment. Eventually, he accepted the truth. Those men would never have let the girl go. Helping her had been right. Defending himself had been necessary. The outcome was tragic but unavoidable. With that settled, he focused on the trail back to the cave.

What he did not know was the story was already spreading. It was the tale of Pale Bear, the large white man who spoke Iroquois and killed two white men to save a Seneca girl.

The girl had reached her camp and breathlessly recounted what had happened to her parents and the leaders. Two of them, Hiawachi and Gray Wolf, returned to the salt site. They found the bodies pulled to the side and followed the tracks east.

Aaron and Red Wolf had stopped to let the horses drink from a stream when Red Wolf motioned for silence. They circled behind the horses and waited.

Hiawachi and Gray Wolf stepped into the clearing. Hiawachi called, "We would speak with Pale Bear."

Aaron stepped forward. "I am Pale Bear."

Hiawachi inclined his head. "I am Hiawachi of the Seneca. My daughter says you saved her life. I thank you."

Aaron answered in Iroquois. "Those men meant her harm. Your daughter is innocent. There was no other choice." He glanced at Red Wolf then back to Hiawachi. "Will you share our food?"

They sat together, eating dried venison, and speaking of the forest, the game, and the rising tensions between the French and the British. They spoke of the tribes who were choosing sides. The Iroquois Confederacy had allied with the British. The Algonquins and Hurons were allied with the French. Hiawachi feared a war was coming, not just between the British and French, but among the tribes themselves. As the southernmost tribe in the Confederacy, he hoped the fighting would stay far to the north, beyond the ridges and valleys the Seneca called home.

When Hiawachi and Gray Wolf left, Red Wolf and Aaron continued east. They camped at the valley's edge, then climbed the ridge the next morning. Two days later, they entered the cave again.

Chapter 9

Norfolk, Virginia 1741

Aaron guessed it was mid-February when Red Wolf decided to go back to Norfolk. This time, they could ride their horses and carry their furs, salt and supplies on the extra pack animals. The return trip was faster; they arrived at the tavern in early March, just in time for the evening meal.

Mary's face lit up when she saw Aaron. She handed him and Red Wolf thick slices of warm bread with butter and jam and tankards of water.

"Thank you, Mary," Aaron said. "I've thought often of your wonderful hot bread and butter."

Mary's smile brightened with pride. Red Wolf watched the exchange and frowned. He feared his sister's daughter would get her heart bruised over Pale Bear, who seemed entirely unaware that Mary, Dancing Rain, had feelings for him.

Red Wolf studied Aaron. He had turned seventeen during their travels, had proven himself when he was in danger, and worked hard. He would make a good husband for Dancing Rain, if Pale Bear could be made to see it.

The next day, Aaron and Red Wolf gave James part of the salt and took some to Edward to sell or trade. Edward paid them for the furs and salt, then handed Aaron an accounting of the money Edward had invested for him. Aaron was pleased with his profits. He reinvested the bulk of his profits with Edward, and spent a modest sum on new clothes and sturdy boots.

On the walk back to the tavern, Red Wolf said, "Have you noticed Dancing Rain?"

"Mary?" Aaron asked. "What about her?"

"She shows you affection. In our people, a girl shows her affection with special food, smiles, and warm looks. Dancing Rain has done all of these. What will you do?"

"Do?" Aaron looked stunned. "What am I supposed to do? In my world the man courts the woman to gain affection. I never thought about Mary as anything but James's daughter and a friend. What does she expect?"

"Nothing," Red Wolf said. "Her gestures are her way of expressing her feelings. If you do not return them, do not encourage her. But be gentle. Her mother is not here to guide her." He grinned. "Besides, James will take your scalp if you hurt her."

Aaron instinctively touched his head. "I have no doubt." He shook his head. "I had no idea. I don't know what to do." Yet he remembered the butterflies in his stomach when Mary smiled at him.

"Do nothing," Red Wolf said. "Be kind, but do not encourage her unless it is your intention to wed."

"M-Marry?" Aaron stuttered. "Me? I'm only seventeen!"

Red Wolf chuckled. "In this world, you are a man. You have proven yourself. You can protect a wife who bears you children."

"Wife? Children?" Aaron asked incredulously. "I'm not ready for that!"

"Then do not encourage Dancing Rain," Red Wolf said calmly. He laughed softly at his young friend. He knew Dancing Rain's feelings, which was why he had worked so hard to teach Pale Bear to survive.

Back at the tavern, Red Wolf said his goodbyes. Mary walked him to the horses.

"I will send you word of your grandparents," Red Wolf said. "If they still live, they will want you to visit again."

Mary's eyes misted. "Let me know." She hugged him. "Thank you for teaching Aaron. He is much more confident this spring than when he arrived."

"Pale Bear is a good man," Red Wolf said. "He would make a good husband, but he is reluctant. He feels he is too young."

Mary blushed. "You are perceptive, Uncle. I know these things about Aaron. In time, he will see me differently. I think, in some ways, he already does."

Red Wolf smiled. "You may be right. I hope so, for your sake." He touched her cheek gently. "Goodbye. I will see you again."

Mary waved as he rode away.

Aaron went upstairs to the room he had been using before leaving with Red Wolf. It was empty except for a bed, a chair, and a washstand. He went back downstairs and pulled Mary to the side.

"I assume you rented my room," he said. "Where are my things?"

Mary smiled. "I have them. Wait here." Mary went into her room and returned with his bag, clothes, shoes, and boots.

"Thank you," Aaron said, heading out the back door.

"Where are you going?" Mary asked.

"To the brewing room. I'm going to take a bath," he said with a grin.

An hour later, Aaron returned to the kitchen, clean and feeling almost civilized again, though the cloth clothes felt strange after months in buckskins.

That evening at dinner, Megan said, "Aaron, you look right handsome in civilized clothing." There was an awkward silence.

"Buckskins are civilized too," Aaron said. "And they're a lot more durable than linen or wool."

Megan smiled. "I meant no insult. I only meant you wouldn't wear buckskins to dinner with a Laird."

Aaron considered her words. "Actually, I think I might."

Megan looked shocked. Edward laughed. "I think you would, too, Aaron. And I think your father would see the humor."

"Father?" Megan asked. "Is your father a Laird, Aaron?"

Aaron nodded. "My father is Neil McNeil, Laird of the McNeil clan."

Megan dropped her fork. Hatred flashed across her face. She rose and left the kitchen without a word.

Edward looked as shocked as the others at the table.

"I'll go check on her," he said and followed her outside. He found her pacing in the back yard.

"Megan! What happened?"

Megan was crying. "I was a McNeil," she said bitterly. "My husband, Paul, farmed my father's land. He improved the house and barns, worked hard, grew profitable crops. My cousin, Elden McNeil coveted it. He convinced the Laird's son, John, to give it to him. John threw coin at us and told us to leave for Virginia. We had nowhere else to go, and Paul died on the journey. I hate everything about the McNeils."

"That's a terrible story," Edward said gently. "And I am so sorry for your loss, but Aaron is innocent. The Laird sent him here because he overheard John and Duncan plotting to have him arrested by the English. He is as much a victim as you are."

Megan frowned. "Victim or not, he's still a McNeil. I cannot let go of my feelings so easily. But, aye, the brothers did not do well by their own. I wish Aaron had been the firstborn. He got the tiny bit of good from the McNeil."

Though her face was still red from crying, she had calmed by the time Edward led her back to the kitchen.

Before sitting, Megan said, "Please excuse my rude behavior." She looked at Aaron, her eyes still flashing with anger. "I was born a McNeil. My husband farmed my father's land. John drove us off because Elden McNeil wanted our crops. It was a shock to learn you are the Laird's son. I did not recognize you. We heard you were missing. I suppose you are."

Aaron looked stricken. "Megan, I am so sorry. Father would never have allowed such a thing. Why did you not appeal to him?"

"John told us if we ever set foot on McNeil land again, we would face consequences," she said, her voice trembling. "We had children. What were we to do?"

Aaron shook his head. "I knew John had a meanness, but not to that extent." He sighed. "I promise you he regrets it now. Elden McNeil is too lazy to farm. He probably thought the crops on your land magically appeared."

"That gives me no comfort," Megan said bitterly. "My children will grow up without their father because a McNeil ran us out of Scotland. I will have to work twice as hard to provide a living and be both parents to my children because a McNeil ran us off our land. You may be a victim, too, but I cannot overlook the fact that you are from the Laird just as John is. Even if you are the best of them, you are still one of them."

Michael, who had been listening, said, "Ma, I miss Da, and I wish he had not died, but I like it better here than where we were."

"Me, too," Emmy echoed.

Megan hugged them. "I know you do. You have a chance here you would never have back in Scotland."

Aaron nodded. "And I would never have been more than a vassal to my brother. This is a good land."

Megan looked at Aaron. Her eyes narrowed, but she gave him a slight nod of acknowledgement.

Aaron took a deep breath. He felt terrible that his brother had caused her husband's death. He had no part in it, but he understood her grief. Maybe one day she could forgive his relationship to John.

CHAPTER 10

Norfolk, Virginia 1741

"Keep her steady!" James called as he watched Aaron plow the field behind the tavern. When the ground had been broken, Aaron smoothed it with a harrow.

"Now, we plant," James said.

Spring warmed the tidewater area of Virginia sooner than the piedmont or mountains, and James always had his garden planted by early April.

The four of them, James, Aaron, Mary, and Megan, worked in practiced rhythm, dropping seeds and covering them with the soft, fragrant soil. They planted oats, barley, onions, corn, squash, beans, carrots, cabbages, okra, and tomatoes. The winter wheat grew beside them.

James held up a handful of seeds. "I got tomato seeds in Italy. The carrots from Persia, the sweet potatoes from Spain, and the other potatoes from Ireland. Seeds are the easiest way to carry food across the ocean."

When the planting was done, James wiped his brow and turned to Aaron. "We are running low on meat. Business is steady in the tavern, and what we have isn't stretching far. Could you see your way to go hunting?"

Aaron nodded. "Aye. I can do that." Before leaving, he set traps in the woods behind the garden for small game.

The next morning, dressed in buckskins and carrying supplies, Aaron ferried across the river. His first stop was the Nottaway village.

Red Wolf stepped from his lodge with a smile. "What brings you here? Are James and Dancing Rain well?"

"They are," Aaron said. "The tavern's doing well, but meat supplies are low. I'm heading out to hunt and thought you might want to come."

"Good idea," Red Wolf said. "We can always use venison." He gathered his rifle and gear, loaded his horse, and joined Aaron as they rode west.

"We cannot make it a long hunt," Red Wolf said quietly. "My father does not have many days left."

Aaron's expression softened. "I'm sorry. Loss is never easy. But James wants me back quickly, too."

The next morning both men brought down a deer. They skinned the animals, cut the meat into strips and smoked them over a fire of green wood. Smoke curled upward, sharp and sweet. As they worked, Red Wolf asked for news.

"The French and Spanish are raiding merchant ships," Aaron said. "James and Edward have been lucky their ships have not been targeted. And more boats of immigrants keep coming."

Red Wolf nodded slowly. "We have our land by treaty, but we are surrounded. Many ask to buy it, but so far, we refuse."

Aaron laid another strip of venison across the rack. "I don't know how all those people survive. I would have died of ignorance if James and then you had not taken me under your wings and taught me."

They were laying more venison across the fire when they heard horses. They got their rifles and blended into the woods.

Three strangers rode into the clearing.

"Food!" one of the men exclaimed. "I'm starving." He swung down from his saddle, approached the fire, and reached for a strip of venison.

Aaron stepped from the woods. Red Wolf stayed hidden.

"That's my kill you're stealing," Aaron said.

"Not stealing," the man said. "Eating."

"Go kill your own deer," Aaron said, walking closer.

The men ignored him and tore into the meat.

Aaron stepped closer. "I said, leave my kill alone."

The first man pulled out a pistol and leveled it at Aaron. "No. We'll eat and take what's left."

For a heartbeat, Aaron felt the cold certainty of danger settle in his chest. Then he moved.

He lunged, knocking the pistol from the man's hand and striking the man hard across the jaw. The other two men jerked up their rifles. A shot cracked from the woods from Red Wolf's rifle. One man fell, his eyes wide with surprise.

Aaron grabbed the other man's rifle and drove his knife beneath his ribs. The man collapsed with a strangled gasp.

The first man staggered to his feet, knife raised. Red Wolf's hatchet struck him in the back, breaking ribs and puncturing a lung. He dropped to his knees, gasping.

Aaron knelt beside him. "Why couldn't you have asked?

I would have fed you and let you be on your way." The man closed his eyes and stopped breathing.

Red Wolf and Aaron stripped the men of valuables and weapons, pulled them into the woods, and left the campsite behind.

At their new camp, Aaron hung the venison over the fire again. The smoke stung his eyes, or perhaps it was anger burning behind them.

"Why can't people be reasonable?" Aaron asked. "I didn't want to kill them, but they were ready to kill me over food I would've shared. All they had to do was ask."

Red Wolf rested a hand on Aaron's shoulder. "Arrogance is an unwise partner with ignorance. Those men had both. You have honor, Pale Bear. They did not. Protect yourself, or you will not live long enough to use that honor."

Aaron nodded, though the tightness in his chest remained. "I know you are right. It still angers me to be forced to kill."

"Do not let your anger rule your mind," Red Wolf said. "Accept truth. You would be dead if you had not fought. You are young. There will be more moments like this. Accept them as part of this world and be ready to protect yourself, and those with you."

Aaron drew a long breath and returned to the meat.

They hunted a few more days, smoking the venison until it was dry and ready to pack.

When they finished, Red Wolf said, "It is time for me to return."

They rode back to the village, parted ways, and Aaron returned to Norfolk.

James met Aaron as he rode in, noting the extra horse loaded with hides and meat. He took the reins.

"Did you buy another horse?" he asked.

"No." Aaron's voice carried a bitterness James had never heard before. "I'm selling it. I don't want to look at it."

James helped him unpack, watching the young man's tightened jaw and distant eyes. Life on the frontier left marks. The extra horse told James enough.

"Are you alright?" James asked.

Aaron nodded, then looked up. Tears glimmered. "All they had to do was ask for food. They didn't have to try and kill me for it."

"They?" James asked.

"Three. Red Wolf killed two."

James understood the rest. He placed his hand on Aaron's shoulder. "Defending yourself is wise, honorable, and natural, but that does not make it easier."

Aaron shook his head. "I killed two men last winter who were trying to kidnap a young Indian girl. I didn't feel like this. Those men were evil. These were just arrogant and stupid. They didn't have to die."

James studied Aaron, and for the first time, he felt a cold prickle of dread. This was no longer the green, inexperienced boy who had arrived from Scotland. He was a man tempered by blood and the harsh realities of the frontier. He was a man who could navigate a Williamsburg parlor as easily as he could kill in the woods. As he watched Aaron, James found his thoughts drifting toward Mary. He saw her growing affection for Aaron. But he wasn't sure if Aaron, with his European education and the heavy burdens he carried, could keep from breaking her heart.

CHAPTER 11

Norfolk, Virginia 1741

Spring eased into summer, and with it came news from the Nottoway village. Red Wolf sent word that Mary's grandfather had died. Sad and wanting to see her grandmother, Mary asked to go to the village when most of the garden had finished bearing its produce. She and James decided Aaron would take her in September.

Edward, having honored Megan's year of mourning, began courting her openly. Megan received his attentions, and before long, they announced their intention to marry. Their ceremony took place after Sunday Services at the Church of England in Norfolk. When Megan moved into Edward's room, it freed a chamber for James to rent.

James and Edward collected lumber and marked off the dimensions for the tavern's addition. Labor was easy to find. Ships from England brought men eager for work and a fresh start. Before long, the addition was finished, and the wall between the two sections was removed. The dining room doubled in size. James and Aaron spent long days building tables and benches for the tavern customers and furniture for the rooms upstairs.

In late July, Edward sat in the expanded dining room with James.

"I'm going to build a house on one of the new streets," Edward said. "Megan and the children will move there with me. Megan and I can concentrate on the warehouse and general store which are growing faster than I expected. The supplies I order from England are gone almost as soon as they arrive. I've commissioned plows, hoes, and scythe blades from the blacksmith and handles from a ship's carpenter who's tired of sailing. I'm buying all the cotton, linen, and wool cloth the local women can weave, plus whatever comes from England. If a French ship docks, I will buy from them, though I don't know how much longer that will last. Tensions are growing between our two countries, and all we want to do is get on with our lives."

"I know," James said. "Sometimes I think the kings should let us commoners help make decisions."

Edward chuckled in agreement. "This business is growing, too. You need to hire more help. Mary and Megan can barely keep up with the work, and it will be too much for Mary when Megan leaves or for Megan when Mary goes to visit her grandmother."

"You're right," James said. "I'll watch the immigrants coming off the ship. A young couple looking for a fresh start would be ideal."

Aaron noticed the venison supplies were starting to get low again. He was getting ready to go hunting when an idea struck him.

"James!" he called.

"Yes, Aaron?"

"Let's put a notice on the board in the market that you will buy venison, pork, beef, or lamb from the farmers. That should keep you in meat instead of my having to be gone for weeks at a time hunting."

"That's a fine idea," James said. He went into his room and brought out a pen, ink, and some paper. "Make your sign and take it there today."

Aaron made the sign and tacked it on the community board in the market. On his way back to the tavern, he saw the masts of a newly arrived ship settling in at the wharf. Many Scots had immigrated that summer. With every ship that docked, he scanned the crowds for any familiar faces, but so far, none had appeared.

By the time he reached the street above the wharf, passengers were already disembarking. He watched for a moment, saw no one he knew, and turned to go back to the tavern.

"Where do we go?" Aaron heard a female voice ask.

"I don't know," the man answered.

Aaron heard the familiar Scottish accent. He turned back around and looked at the couple.

"Gordon!" Aaron exclaimed. "Gordon McNeil?"

The young man looked up. "Aye. I'm Gordon McNeil. Who are you?"

Aaron grinned. "Aaron McNeil! You likely don't recognize me. I was a small, puny lad when Father sent me here."

"The Laird sent you here?" Gordon asked, astonished. "Why?"

Aaron's smile faded. "My brothers were going to have

me arrested by the British for smuggling. They wanted rid of me. Father found out and sent me here."

"You vanished, and no one knew what to think," Gordon said. "Some believed you were murdered. The Laird looks sad these days. I think he misses you."

"I miss him," Aaron said softly. "But it is good here. I can be more than a vassal to John." He nodded toward the woman beside Gordon.

"This is my wife, Blair," Gordon said. "We saved for the passage. There is nothing for us in Scotland but hard work and no thanks for it. Here we can make our own way."

"Come with me," Aaron said. "I'll get you some food."

He led them to the tavern, walked in, and saw James.

"James! This is Gordon McNeil and his wife, Blair. They are kinsmen from Scotland, just off the ship."

James smiled. "Nice to meet you." He looked at Aaron. "I'm guessing you want food for them. Go tell Mary."

He turned to the newcomers. "Have a seat. Aaron will be right back."

James stood back and watched Aaron talk with the couple while they ate. After a while, he approached them.

"Gordon, what are your plans?"

Gordon sighed. "We had no plans beyond getting here. That alone felt like an accomplishment."

James nodded. "I could use help. I will give you a room and your food plus a shilling each per month. There's more work than we can manage now. Megan is moving soon, and Mary will be visiting her grandmother in September."

Gordon and Blair exchanged a look of relief.

"We'll take your offer, Mr. Montgomery," Gordon said.

"We're grateful."

"Call me James," he said warmly. He led them upstairs to the vacant room near the back stairs, next to Aaron's. "This is your room. Go ahead and get settled in."

Then he led them down the back stairs to the kitchen. He introduced them to Megan, Mary, Michael and Emmy. He wasn't surprised to learn that Gordon and Blair already knew Megan and were sad to learn of Paul's death.

James looked at the group in the kitchen. "Gordon and Blair, you will meet my nephew, Edward, tonight. Mary, you can get Blair started. Aaron, you take Gordon with you."

By supper, the new McNeil family had already been folded into the Montgomery household. The tavern bustled as it always did when a ship arrived. The Montgomerys and McNeils ate as time allowed, weaving the newcomers into the rhythm of life at the Running Hare.

August settled over Norfolk with heavy heat and long, bright days. The tavern bustled more than ever. With Gordon and Blair learning quickly, James finally had enough hands to keep the work manageable. Mary trained Blair in the kitchen, and the two women moved together with an easy rhythm that made the long days lighter.

Aaron spent much of his time hauling barrels, repairing tables, and helping Gordon learn the ropes of brewing and running the tavern. Yet every time he passed Mary, he felt a tug in his chest, a reminder of Red Wolf's words. He tried to ignore it, but the awareness lingered.

One evening, as the sun dipped low and the tavern quieted, Mary stepped outside to cool off. Aaron was stacking firewood near the back door. She paused beside him.

"Father says we can leave for the village in September," she said softly. "Grandmother will be alone now. I want to spend a few weeks with her."

Aaron nodded. "Aye. I'll take you. We'll leave as soon as the weather turns cooler."

Mary hesitated then added, "Thank you, Aaron. I know you are busy, but this means a great deal to me."

Her voice carried a tenderness that made his stomach flutter. He looked away, unsure what to do with the warmth rising in his chest.

"'Tis no trouble," he said quietly. "I'd not have you travel alone."

Mary smiled and went back inside.

By the middle of September, the grains had been harvested, and Aaron prepared to take Mary to her grandmother. He was eager to see Red Wolf again. His horses would make the journey quicker than the one they'd taken the year before.

On the morning of their departure, Aaron came downstairs in his buckskins.

Gordon stared. "Aaron, you look like a mountain man! I had no idea you had such clothes."

Aaron smiled. "A gift from Mary's Nottoway kin. They're warm and durable."

Mary stepped from her room wearing moccasins, buckskin leggings and a long buckskin shirt that nearly reached her knees.

Aaron blinked in surprise. "I didn't know you had those!"

Mary smiled. "My grandparents gave them to me the day we left last year. I wanted grandmother to see me wearing them. Besides, they are perfect for riding."

They mounted their horses, waved goodbye, and rode toward the Nottoway village. After crossing the river by ferry, they followed the well-traveled road, talking easily. But once they turned onto the woodland trail, the forest quieted them. They stopped once to rest and water the horses, then continued on. Evening shadows stretched long across the ground when they entered the village.

Red Wolf greeted them with a wide smile. Mary hugged him, then hurried to her grandmother's lodge. Aaron followed more slowly.

Inside, the elderly woman, Rain Flower, held Mary's hand. Their voices were low and tender. When Rain Flower saw Aaron, she motioned him closer. He hesitated, puzzled, but obeyed and sat on the ground next to Mary.

Rain Flower spoke in soft, measured Iroquois. "I had a vision. In my vision, I saw mountains, a cave, a waterfall, and a cabin. Wheat and oats grew there, and the three sisters. Dancing Rain worked in the garden and cooked in the cabin." She took Mary's hand and placed it in Aaron's. "Pale Bear was there. He grew the grain, trapped the furs and worked in the cave. Pale Bear and Dancing Rain will live there together."

Aaron froze when he felt Mary's warm fingers against his.

Rain Flower continued, her voice growing weak. "I will not see this. My vision says I will see my Running Wolf before the leaves fall." She cupped Mary's face. "My sweet granddaughter. Daughter of my daughter, you will work hard, but you will be happy and prosperous." She took Aaron's hand. "Pale Bear, you will save many. White men and Iroquois will look to you for help and wisdom."

She folded their clasped hands between her own. "This is the vision the spirits gave me before my death. I can go to them in peace." Rain Flower lay back on the furs and closed her eyes.

Aaron stared at Mary's hand still resting in his. Shock rippled through him.

Mary saw his discomfort, squeezed his hand gently, and said, "You can go outside. I will sit with Grandmother for a while."

Aaron nodded and stepped out of the lodge, dazed. Red Wolf saw his expression and laughed.

"Pale Bear, what has you so shaken?"

Aaron looked back at the lodge. "Is a vision before death common among the Nottoway?"

Red Wolf smiled. "No. Father did not have one. He would be jealous to know Mother did."

Aaron ran a hand through his hair. "She practically said I was going to marry Mary. What if Mary doesn't want that? What if I am not ready to marry?"

Red Wolf grinned. "You think too much. Did Rain Flower say when this would happen?"

"No."

"Then it will happen when the time is right, if it happens at all," Red Wolf said calmly. "A vision is not a chain. The future is not fixed until it becomes the past." He motioned to a woman who brought Aaron a bowl of stew.

"Eat," Red Wolf said. "It is easier to think about the future if you are not hungry."

Aaron gave him a look that clearly said, "Have you lost

your mind?" Red Wolf burst into laughter.

Aaron sat on the ground outside Red Wolf's lodge and ate, though his thoughts churned. Rain Flower had spoken as though his future was already written. How did he feel about that? He had never held Mary's hand before, yet he had liked the warmth of it.

Red Wolf joined him. "Did you recognize the land in Rain Flower's vision?"

"Yes, it was where we went hunting."

"You liked that place," Red Wolf said. "Perhaps this is why. Some things cannot be explained, visions among them." It was getting dark. "Get some rest. We hunt tomorrow."

Aaron nodded and returned to the longhouse, settling in the same place he had slept the year before.

The next morning Red Wolf shot a deer. Aaron helped him drain the blood and carry it back to the village. They skinned it, and the women divided the meat.

"We were lucky," Red Wolf said. "The buffalo and elk are gone. Even the deer grow fewer. Soon we will be eating only squirrel and rabbit with our vegetables."

"James cannot keep meat either," Aaron said. "He finally started buying from farmers. He enlarged the tavern, and it fills up when a ship comes in."

"Dancing Rain's father is wise in business," Red Wolf said.

"So is Edward," Aaron said. "He took my investment in the company and increased it greatly. I may need it to buy the land in Rain Flower's vision."

Red Wolf raised an eyebrow. "So you believe it now?"

"I am not dismissing it," Aaron said. "You were right

when you said I liked the land. And it's intriguing, thinking I may make part of her vision real."

"And Dancing Rain?"

Aaron hesitated. "Rain Flower put an idea in my head that wasn't there before. I'm not ready to decide anything."

Red Wolf's gaze sharpened. "Dancing Rain heard the vision, too. She already has feelings for you. This will deepen them. Be careful with her heart."

"I know. That's what frightens me," Aaron said softly. "I would never want to hurt Mary. She's... special. I've always thought that. Maybe that's the beginning of something. We'll see."

CHAPTER 12

Scottish Hebrides 1741

Ian MacNeil finished reading the letter from his daughter, Megan. Relief washed through him; she was safe in Virginia. But anger followed quickly. Paul was dead, and John MacNeil was the cause of it. His joints protested as he rose from his chair. He needed to speak to an old friend.

Neil MacNeil was at his brother Fletcher's brewing house when Ian arrived. Fletcher was reminiscing.

"Aaron was a natural brewer," Fletcher said. "I hated to lose him."

"It was for the best," Neil replied.

Fletcher shook his head. "He was the best of us. Scotland needs men like he would have been."

A knock sounded at the door. Fletcher brightened. "Ian! Come in!"

Neil smiled at the sight of his old companion. The three of them had once been inseparable. They were young, reckless, and always in trouble.

"It's good to see you, Ian," Neil said.

"And you," Ian said. "But I need a word with the Laird."

Neil's expression tightened. "Of course. Let's walk."

They stepped outside, following the path toward Fletcher's house.

"What troubles you?" Neil asked.

"I received a letter from Megan," Ian said.

"Letter?" Neil stopped. "Where is she?"

"You don't know?" Ian asked quietly.

Neil shook his head. "Tell me. All of it."

Ian told Neil everything. Elden's greed. John's willingness to evict Megan and Paul. The forced passage to Virginia. John's threats if they returned. Paul's death at sea. Megan and the children finding refuge with Aaron in Norfolk.

"They're doing well, now," Ian said. "I honestly think the children are happier there, and they will certainly have better futures there. But you needed to know what John has done. He is indirectly responsible for Paul's death."

Neil exhaled slowly, feeling sick to his stomach. "Thank you for telling me. Why did you not come to me then? I would have straightened everything out, including my son. I wonder how many more of the clan have been harmed by him."

"No one is going to tell you, Neil, because they're afraid of John. He has most of the clan fearful that they will lose their farms at any moment."

Sadness and guilt washed over Neil. He had trusted John, but that trust was gone now.

Neil inhaled deeply. "I would ask that you keep the information of Aaron's location to yourself. Fletcher knows he is in Virginia, but only you and I know where. I sent him away because of John, but I didn't think John would turn on the clan."

When Ian turned to go home, Neil clasped his arm. "Thank you for your honesty. I cannot undo what has happened, but I can make sure it does not happen again."

Neil watched his friend walk back to his cottage. He returned to Fletcher's house, said goodbye, and had his men row him back to the castle.

That evening at supper, Neil said, "John, I heard today that Paul Brown has died."

John hesitated, only a heartbeat, but Neil saw it.

"I did not know that," John said.

"I went by his farm," Neil continued. "Why are there more weeds than grain? Paul was one of our best farmers."

"I don't know. I will check on it tomorrow."

"No," Neil said. "We both know why the farm is failing. You took it from a good man and gave it to Elden, who is lazy. What did Elden offer you to make it worth evicting the Browns?"

John flushed. Neil noticed it.

"It must have been a delicate matter," Neil said, "or something you now regret, if it makes you blush." He sighed. "I will oversee the farms myself until after the harvest."

John bristled. "You don't need to do that."

"Oh, I do," Neil replied. "Your tenants need reassurance they will not lose their farms." Neil rose and left the room.

John's anger simmered. Only Ian could have told Neil. Ian would pay for it.

The next morning Neil noticed John was not at breakfast. He asked the men at the table where John was. One answered that he had crossed the channel early and was on the mainland.

"I need to go to the mainland," Neil said, already walking toward the door. "Now!"

Minutes later, Neil was in a boat, and his men were rowing hard across the narrow channel. On the mainland, he mounted a horse and rode straight to Ian's cottage. The door stood open.

Inside, the cottage was destroyed. Furniture was overturned and pottery shattered. In the back of the cottage, Ian lay on the floor, unconscious.

"Bring him to Fletcher's," Neil ordered, his voice cold.

Neil rode to Fletcher's manor house and burst through the door. "Fletcher!"

Fletcher came running out of his study. "What's wrong?"

"Ian McNeil has been badly beaten," Neil said. "Will you let him recover here?"

"Of course." Fletcher turned and told one of the servants to get the doctor in town.

"What happened?" Fletcher asked.

"I don't know. Hopefully, Ian will tell us, but I'm afraid it was John. I confronted John about the Browns last night. I assume John realized that the only way I could have found out was through Ian."

The door opened and the men carried Ian inside on a makeshift stretcher. The housekeeper took them to a room that was easily accessible by staff. The doctor came and examined Ian, who was still unconscious.

"Will he live?" Neil asked.

"I cannot say," the doctor replied. "It depends on internal bleeding. I can set the broken bones in his arm and leg, but I cannot determine the head injury while he sleeps. I'll know more when he wakes."

Neil sat by Ian's bed for hours, until Ian's eyes fluttered open. He groaned.

Neil leaned forward. "Ian, you're safe at Fletcher's. Who did this?"

Ian's jaw tightened. "John."

Neil nodded. "Rest and get well. I will deal with John."

Back at the castle, Neil stormed into the great hall.

"Where's your brother?" he demanded of Duncan.

"He left," Duncan said. "Rome. He's joining the Stuarts. He plans to return with James when the throne is restored."

"Did you know what he did to the Browns?" Neil asked.

"Aye," Duncan admitted. "I told him it was wrong, but he listens to no one. He acts as if he is already Laird."

"Did he harm anyone else?" Neil asked.

"Not like that. He mostly made the clan fearful. I tried to calm them, but they knew I had no power."

"Did you know about Ian McNeil?" Neil asked.

Duncan's face turned pale. "What happened?"

"He was beaten nearly to death this morning," Neil said. "I'm not sure he will live. He regained consciousness long enough to tell me it was John."

Duncan looked horrified. "I didn't know!"

Neil placed a hand on his shoulder. "I'm glad you knew nothing of it. It must have been the last thing John did before fleeing."

"Ian?" Duncan muttered, stunned. "Ian taught me to fish in the river. Where is he?"

"He's at Fletcher's," Neil said as he led Duncan to his study.

"From now on, you and I will work together to repair what John has damaged." Neil paused. "I am going to tell you something, but you must swear never to repeat it."

"I swear," Duncan said.

"Aaron is in Virginia. I heard you and John plotting against him, so I sent him away to save his life."

Duncan's eyes widened. "Father, I would have never let John harm him. You must believe that. I listen and agree with John, but I do my best to thwart his sometimes evil plans. John is evil, Father. That is the only word to describe him."

Neil nodded. "Keep a bag packed and coin hidden. If I am dead when John returns, go to Virginia. Aaron is in Norfolk at a place called the Running Hare Tavern. And do not join the Stuart cause. If James wins, leave. If he loses, stay and see what becomes of John."

Neil turned and reached for a ledger. "Now, we will work together to run the estate."

John MacNeil stood at the rail of a ship bound for France, watching Scotland shrink into the gray horizon. The sight pleased him. Before leaving, he had left his mark, Ian's broken body lying on the floor of his cottage. It would remind the clan what happened to those who crossed him. They needed to fear him.

Marseille awaited him, and with it, the Jacobite men who would recognize his worth far better than his own family ever had. From there, he would travel to Rome, to the court of King James III, where true power gathered. John imagined himself among them, finally seen, finally valued, finally above the petty constraints of Skye. And when he did return to Skye, he would not come back as a son. He would return as a man his father could no longer command. He would be a man his father would have to bow to.

CHAPTER 13

Virginia Tidewater Region 1741

Aaron and Mary had been at the village a week when Rain Flower died. Mary grieved, but she was grateful she had been at her grandmother's side when she passed into the land of the spirits. After Rain Flower was laid to rest beside her husband, Aaron and Mary said goodbye to Red Wolf and began the journey back to Norfolk.

They rode along the trail in silence. Aaron could see tears running down Mary's cheeks. He understood her grief. Not only had she lost both grandparents, she had lost her place and her automatic acceptance in the village. Without a reason to visit, people and relatives would forget her. Finally her tears dried, and she looked at Aaron.

"We have not spoken of Grandmother's vision. Were you shocked?"

Aaron laughed. "Shocked is too mild a word. Try completely bewildered."

Mary smiled. "She surprised me, too. Do you know the land she spoke of?"

"Yes," Aaron said. "It's where Red Wolf and I camped last winter while trapping."

"Did you like it?" Mary asked.

"I did. I thought it would make a fine homestead."

Mary nodded thoughtfully. "That is good to know. If you liked it, I would like it. Now the hard question. What did you think about her saying we lived there together?"

"That's the part that has me bewildered," Aaron admitted. Mary laughed, and he smiled. "I like you, Mary. Truly. But I never let myself think of you as any more than James's daughter." He glanced at her. "What did you think?"

Mary's smile was soft. "I was a little surprised, but not like you were. I have thought for a long time that you would make a good husband."

"You did?" he asked.

"Yes. Do you not think so?"

"I've never considered myself in those terms," he said. "Back home, I would be going to a university, not thinking about marriage. Here, everything happens so fast. One moment you're a child, and the next minute you are fighting to stay alive. And people. One minute you have your family and friends around you, and the next minute a loved one is dead or missing." Aaron paused. "The last thing I want is to hurt you. So, perhaps we should think about what Rain Flower said but take our time. I will say this." He glanced at her. "I believe you would make a wonderful wife."

"A wonderful wife?" Mary teased.

"Yes. I used the word wonderful," he said and saw her smile. Her smile warmed him more than the sun on the trail.

They rode in silence for a while before Aaron asked, "Mary, how old are you?"

"Sixteen."

"When was your birthday?"

"Christmas Day," she answered.

Aaron nodded. "Mine is January 1st. They're a week apart."

They continued through the woods until Aaron raised his hand for silence. Voices drifted ahead on the trail. Aaron guided his horse off the path, and Mary followed. They tethered the horses and slipped into the trees.

Two men rode past, talking loudly.

"I'm tellin' ya, Amos, Jep and Harry should have been back months ago. Somethin's happened. I jist know it."

"Nah," Amos replied. "Jep's too smart. He knows the wilderness better than anyone."

Aaron hoped the men would pass by without stopping, but one of the horses gave a nervous snort. Aaron winced. The men stopped.

"I heard a horse," Amos said looking around. He saw the two horses standing just off the trail and grinned. "Looks like we got ourselves two new horses!"

The two men dismounted and approached the animals.

"I know this one!" Amos said. "This is Jep's horse! He must be around here somewhere." He called out. "Jep! Jep, it's Amos." Amos started to untie the horses.

"Leave the horses alone," Aaron called from the trees.

The men froze, looking around. Amos nervously reached for the reins again.

Aaron stepped into view. "I said leave the horses alone."

"Who are you?" Amos demanded. "And why do you

have my brother's horse?"

"My name is John," Aaron said evenly. "I don't know your brother, but the man who owned that horse is dead. He died at the salt flats. I saw it. I was there."

"Who killed him?" Amos asked.

"The man he tried to kill first."

Amos's eyes narrowed, gauging the situation. There were two of them and only one man in buckskins, but there were two horses.

Aaron saw the second man start edging quietly around the horses.

"Who's with you?" Amos asked.

"No one," Aaron replied.

"You have two saddled horses," Amos said.

"I'm delivering it to its new owner."

Aaron watched Amos. At the same time, he watched the other man in his side vision.

Amos kept talking, trying to distract Aaron. "How did my brother die?"

Aaron rested a hand on his hatchet, his mind assessing. One path out. Mary hidden in the trees. One man in front, hand twitching on his rifle. One man behind. He didn't look. He didn't need to. He listened. Boots scraped the dirt, searching for balance, getting closer. Instead of the click of a rifle being cocked, he felt the cold barrel touch the back of his head.

Amos smiled. "Looks like this ain't your lucky day."

Aaron felt the shift in the man's posture behind him, the tightening that meant the shot was coming. He moved before the man could act. In one swift motion, Aaron spun, seized the rifle, and tore it from the man's hands. Using the momentum, he swung the stock in a sharp arc that struck Amos in the head hard enough to send him to his knees.

The hatchet was already in his other hand as Aaron kept moving. The sharp corner of his hatchet opened the throat of the man behind him. He kept turning and saw Amos lifting a pistol.

Amos extended his arm, aiming the pistol toward Aaron. Aaron quickly lifted the hatchet and brought it down on Amos's arm. The bone was severed, and the pistol dropped to the ground.

Amos screamed and held his arm, unable to stop the flow of blood. He looked at Aaron in disbelief, realizing too late that this was the end.

"That is how your brother died," Aaron said sadly. "All you had to do was keep moving."

When the forest fell silent, Aaron's shoulders sagged. The men were dead. He would never get used to this, to the necessity of killing to stay alive. This land might offer opportunity, but out here in the wilderness, there was no law but survival.

A hand touched his arm. He jumped, then saw it was Mary.

"Are you alright?" she asked. "Are you hurt?"

Aaron shook his head. "No. I am unharmed. Why did they try to kill me? They could have just kept going. I don't like hurting anyone, and I especially don't like killing."

"You saved your life and mine," Mary said. "There is nothing dishonorable about that. You were brave and quick. Had you been killed..." Mary swallowed. "I hate to think what would have happened."

Aaron pulled her into a hug. "Are you alright? I did not think to ask."

"I'm fine," she said, wrapping her arms around him. "I'm proud of you. Thank you for keeping me safe."

Mary made him feel strong and brave. He liked keeping her safe, and he liked that she was proud of him. His thoughts were so jumbled, he hadn't realized he was still holding her until he became aware he liked holding her. And she hadn't pulled away.

He leaned down and kissed her. His reaction startled him. He wanted to get closer.

Mary's arms slipped around Aaron's neck, and she kissed him back with equal intensity. She had loved him for months.

Aaron pulled away, breathless. "Mary? Are you angry with me?"

Mary shook her head, then pulled him back for another kiss. "I will only be angry if you never want to do that again."

Aaron laughed softly. "Maybe Rain Flower knew what she was talking about." Aaron released her. "We had better go."

They returned to the horses. Aaron stripped the men of money, valuables, and weapons, then led the extra horses to Norfolk.

James was in the tavern yard when they arrived. He took the reins of the extra horses, raising an eyebrow.

"They attacked first," Aaron said as he dismounted. James nodded.

"Were you hurt?" James asked Mary.

Mary shook her head. "I hid in the woods. Aaron handled both men before they could react."

Mary watched Aaron take the horses to the barn, then

turned back to James.

"Father, I have never seen any man move like Aaron did. He waited, absolutely still, until the exact moment he needed to act. Then it was over in less than a minute. But he didn't strike first. He didn't even raise a hand until one man put the barrel of his rifle against Aaron's head."

James looked toward the barn where Aaron had disappeared. He believed Mary. He'd seen enough of Aaron to know the boy carried a kind of competence that didn't come from training alone. It came from hardship, necessity, and a maturity that was older than his years.

"Father," Mary said, drawing his attention back to her. "You should know that I am going to marry Aaron."

"Did he ask you?" James asked.

"Not yet. But he will," Mary said smiling and went into the kitchen.

James stood there, stunned.

"Is something wrong?" Aaron asked as he came out of the barn.

James looked at him and shook his head. "That girl flusters me."

Aaron laughed. "Me, too," he said and followed her inside.

CHAPTER 14

Norfolk, Virginia 1741

Aaron walked through the busy Norfolk market, weaving past wagons and crates that sat along the street. He stopped by a cart where a woman was selling pumpkins. Her hands, still dusty from the field, gratefully took his coins when he bought two.

Mary looked up when he entered the kitchen. "Pumpkins! Where did you get them? Ours are still green."

"In the market," Aaron said. "As soon as I saw them, I thought to myself that Mary would like to have some pumpkins." He grinned.

Mary laughed. "More like Aaron wanted pumpkin pudding."

"Have I had your pumpkin pudding?" Aaron asked, teasing her. She had made several the year before. "Is it good?"

Mary rolled her eyes. "I guess I'll make one, and you can decide for yourself." She tapped one of the pumpkins. "Thank you for thinking of me." A hint of sarcasm edged her voice, then her laugh followed, light and warm.

Aaron realized how much he liked the sound of her laughter. He paused, his expression softening.

"The woman selling them looked hungry," he said. "I couldn't resist giving her the coin."

Mary smiled at him. "You're kind, Aaron. It will make the pumpkin pudding all the more special."

That evening, as the group settled in for a meal, Aaron smiled as he tasted the pumpkin pudding. Mary smiled back. His act of kindness made it all the sweeter. Life was hard for farmers in the Virginia Tidewater. He was glad he had helped the woman.

In early November, Red Wolf rode into the backyard of the tavern. Aaron had just stepped out of the brewing room.

"Red Wolf!" he called.

Red Wolf smiled. "Pale Bear, it is good to see you." They clasped arms in greeting.

"What brings you to Norfolk?" Aaron asked.

"Would you like to go back to the mountains? We need meat and salt."

Aaron grinned. "Yes. When do you want to leave?"

"As soon as you can be ready." The two men walked into the kitchen.

Mary looked up and smiled. "Uncle! It is good to see you." She went over and hugged Red Wolf. She looked over to see Blair staring.

"Blair, this is my uncle, Red Wolf."

"H-hello," she stammered.

Red Wolf smiled and in perfect English said, "Hello, Blair. Nice to meet you."

Mary set a bowl of stew and a tankard of cool water

before him. "Have some food, Uncle. I know your trip here has made you hungry."

Red Wolf grinned. "Thank you, Dancing Rain."

Mary picked up a stack of clean linens. "I'll just take these upstairs."

Red Wolf watched her go, smiled, and said in Iroquois, "I'll be here. You can tell Pale Bear to take his time."

Mary blushed. "I'll tell him."

Red Wolf laughed, and Blair looked utterly confused.

Aaron had changed into his buckskins when Mary came down the hall. He looked around, saw no one and pulled her into his arms. Her softness contrasted to his rough hands. He felt his pulse quicken as he kissed her.

"I will miss you," he said.

"I will miss you, too. Make it a short trip."

He held her close and kissed her again. "Don't start thinking about any of those other Norfolk boys while I'm gone."

Mary laughed. "Then you'd better hurry back so my mind won't wander."

Aaron growled playfully, hugged her hard and kissed her again. "You go down first. I'll follow."

Mary walked back into the kitchen to find Red Wolf sitting at the table with James and grinning at her.

"What?" Mary asked.

They grinned wider. Mary looked past the men to see Blair pointing to her hair.

Mary frowned and touched the back of her head. Her hair had come loose. She rolled her eyes and fixed it.

Aaron walked into the room wearing his buckskins. The hatchet and hunting knife were attached to his belt, and he carried his rifle.

He looked at James. "What do you want me to bring back besides furs and salt?"

"Any smoked meat Red Wolf can spare, but he may need it all. I can buy meat in the market."

Aaron nodded to Red Wolf. "I'll get my horses ready." A few minutes later, he returned. "I'm ready. We can stop by the warehouse for empty salt sacks."

Mary handed them a cloth bundle filled with bread, jerky, and apples.

"Thank you, Dancing Rain," Red Wolf said.

"Thanks, Mary," Aaron said.

The men mounted their horses and led their pack horses out of the yard. Mary waved them off.

James looked at Mary. "Did he ask you?"

Mary smiled. "Not yet, but he's getting closer." She kissed James on the cheek and went back to work.

CHAPTER 15

Virginia Wilderness 1741

On the trail, Red Wolf said, "I saw you had two more horses."

Aaron nodded. "Aye. We ran into some trouble on the way back from your village."

"Was Dancing Rain hurt?" Red Wolf asked.

"No. They did not even know she was around," Aaron said. "Turns out one of them was the brother of one of the men at the salt flats last winter." He shook his head. "Meanness must run in the family."

Red Wolf chuckled, the sound echoing through the trees. Then his expression shifted.

"I see affection between you and Mary."

"Yes. It is there," Aaron said. "We are not rushing, but I do plan to marry her, and she plans to marry me. We just have to decide when we are ready."

Red Wolf smiled. "I am glad. You are right for each other."

"I want to buy the property where you hunt," Aaron said. "It was in Rain Flower's vision. I like the area, and the Nottoway will always be welcome to hunt and trap there."

"I think that is wise. It is good land. Not too steep, and surrounded by higher peaks. But you will be isolated for a long time, until the roads through the mountains are better."

Aaron shrugged. "That's all right. As long as I can get my furs and crops down the mountain to sell, I'll be fine."

They rode on. The forest swallowed the sound of the horses' hooves, and a gentle breeze carried the scent of pine and damp earth. Red Wolf turned off the main road onto a forest path.

"We are going to the village," Aaron said. "Do you need to get supplies?"

Red Wolf grinned. "A few, but I need to get Running Bear." Running Bear was Red Wolf's son.

Aaron grinned. "Will this be his first long hunt?"

"Yes. It is time."

"Good," Aaron said nodding. "He needs to know where the camp is. When I own it, and after Mary and I are married, it will be family land for both the McNeils and Nottoways."

Red Wolf shook his head with a quiet smile. "Rain Flower was right. If things go as you wish, you will be valuable to both white men and Iroquois."

Aaron smiled. "I don't know about valuable, but I'd like to be a blessing to people."

They rode into the village. Running Bear was already mounted, waiting with anticipation. As soon as they emerged from the woods, he urged his horse forward, leading Red Wolf's pack horse by the reins. Red Wolf nodded his approval to his son, and the three began their journey.

They followed the same trail as the year before, but Aaron noticed more land had been cleared. The path was becoming more of a road. The sight made him anxious to buy the mountain property before someone else could own it. The thought of owning land still felt unreal, like a dream he hadn't dared speak aloud a year ago. It was a dream he never could have reached had he stayed in Scotland.

The third night's camp was at the foot of the mountains. They rested and began the climb at dawn. Even using gaps between the peaks, the trail was grueling. They had to walk and lead the horses several times because it was steep.

On the seventh day, they reached the cave. Red Wolf had Running Bear hold the vines back. Aaron crouched and pointed to the large prints on the cave floor.

"Our bear is back."

After leading the horses to the large room behind the waterfall, Red Wolf lit the fire behind the stone wall in the room. With torches in hand, Red Wolf and Aaron followed the bear's tracks. Running Bear stayed close behind, alert and silent.

The paw prints were larger than before, evidence the animal had grown over the summer. They followed the tunnel that led upward until the odor of bear became overpowering. They stopped, placed the torches on a ledge, and cocked their rifles.

A roar exploded from the shadows. The bear charged.

Red Wolf and Aaron fired; the shots reverberated through the stone chamber. The bear stumbled but didn't slow. Aaron grabbed his hatchet, bracing himself against the powerful blow he knew was coming. The bear reared, claws flashing in the torchlight.

A rifle sounded. The bear collapsed with a heavy thud that echoed through the cave.

Red Wolf and Aaron spun around. Running Bear was standing with his rifle still raised. His breath was quick, and his hands trembled slightly.

Aaron grinned. "This kill goes to Running Bear!"

Running Bear lowered the rifle. Shock flickered across his face, giving way to pride.

Red Wolf stepped beside Running Bear and placed a steady hand on his shoulder. "Well done, Running Bear. The hide is yours."

The boy's grin spread slowly as he realized the prize he would be taking back to the village.

Aaron set up his portable drying racks while Red Wolf taught Running Bear how to skin the bear. By the time the hide was ready, Aaron had fires smoldering in the large cavern, their smoke drifting upward to vent through the tunnels. The work was grueling and repetitive. They sliced the meat into thin strips and layered them over the heat, then constantly tended the fires to ensure the venison dried without spoiling.

Aaron took some of the meat, fried it and made a hearty stew with the leather britches he had brought. Their hunger satisfied, the work continued.

Running Bear yawned, and Red Wolf allowed the boy to go to sleep. Aaron felt the same weariness, but there was still work to do. Fresh meat had to be cooked or dried before it spoiled. A few hours later, Aaron told Red Wolf to get some sleep. Through the night, as the strips on the rack shrank with dehydration, Aaron moved them closer together and added new strips.

When the sky began to lighten, Red Wolf woke Running Bear. Together they went out of the cave and brought back more green wood and smaller branches to build another rack. Soon two fires were smoking meat.

"I wonder if you can smell this meat or see the smoke from the hole in the ground," Aaron said.

"Why don't you go check," Red Wolf said. "We will watch the fires."

After a breakfast of fried meat and the last of the biscuits, Aaron lit a torch and scouted the tunnels to ensure the smoke was venting properly. He found the smoke lingered in the room where the bear had been sleeping but dissipated halfway to the third room beneath the hole. Satisfied the cave would remain hidden, he returned.

The next few days were a blur of labor. They worked night and day smoking the rest of the bear, processing the hides, and even bringing in more venison to ensure their supplies would last into the spring. Fatigue began to show itself in reduced conversation and slower movements.

Still, Aaron found time to continue teaching Red Wolf to read and write. He tried to teach Running Bear, but the boy only stared into space, not listening. Aaron could tell this did not please Red Wolf.

By the time the meat was dry, and the panniers on the horses were full of dried meat, Running Bear was quiet and sullen.

Red Wolf packed his horse and looked at Aaron. "It's time to go get salt."

CHAPTER 16

Early the next morning, Aaron, Red Wolf, and Running Bear packed their gear and left the cave. On the third day, they cautiously approached the salt flats. From the trees, they watched a group filling sacks with salt.

Aaron grinned and pointed to the leader. "It's Hiawachi."

Aaron and Red Wolf walked out of the woods; Running Bear trailed behind them.

The Seneca men quickly raised their rifles, but Hiawachi said, "They are friends."

He greeted Aaron and Red Wolf, and Red Wolf introduced Running Bear. Everyone returned to their work. When all the sacks were filled, the three men exchanged news.

While they talked, a young girl approached Hiawachi. He smiled and said, "This is my daughter, Shining Moon. She wishes to speak with Pale Bear."

Aaron smiled at the girl.

Shining Moon said, "I would thank you for your bravery and saving me from those men."

Aaron smiled and replied in her language, "You are

welcome, Shining Moon. I am glad you are alive and well."

She smiled and returned to her mother. Aaron noticed she kept stealing glances at Running Bear. He smiled. There would be time for teasing later.

That evening the salt flats were empty. It was as if in a long ago history, the tribes agreed to share the salt, but no one would camp there and control the area. Red Wolf, Aaron, and Running Bear sat near a fire and ate the venison jerky.

"I believe Shining Moon was making eyes at Running Bear," Aaron said.

"Do you?" Red Wolf asked, joining the teasing. "A marriage between the Seneca and Nottoway would be advantageous."

"I agree," Aaron said. "Maybe you should look into that. You would be happy to marry a Seneca woman, right Running Bear?" Aaron laughed when Running Bear shot him a look that clearly meant *you're crazy.*

Two nights later, they camped in the cave. The next morning, they left wood behind the stone wall to dry for the next time they needed a fire and started the journey home. By noon five days later, they rode into the Nottoway village. Running Bear's friends greeted him eagerly. Aaron smiled as Running Bear showed them the hide and told the story of the charging bear.

"It was a good hunt, Red Wolf," Aaron said. "Thank you for letting me come."

"You are always welcome, Pale Bear," Red Wolf said. "Do not forget to invite me to your wedding."

Aaron laughed. "I wouldn't dream of getting married without you there, and neither would Mary. I will see you again soon." Aaron turned his horses and started the ride to Norfolk.

Running Bear came up beside Red Wolf. "I am glad he is gone."

Red Wolf looked at him sharply. "Why is that?"

Running Bear snarled, "He's just a stupid white man who tries to be like us. Why do you let him be your friend?"

Red Wolf's eyes hardened. "Would you be so prejudiced that you cannot see a good man and a good friend?"

"Pale Bear?" Running Bear scoffed. "He is no friend. He relies on you for survival in the wilderness and takes credit for our hunt."

"Pale Bear taught you the writing of the white men," Red Wolf said, watching his son closely. "He would not do that if he were not a friend."

"I do not need the white man's letters," Running Bear said. "Nottoway can live without them."

"You are foolish Running Bear," Red Wolf said. "The only way to stay ahead of the white man and not be cheated is to know their language, writings, and numbers. Besides, Pale Bear will be getting married to Dancing Rain. He will be family."

Running Bear snorted. "He's a white man marrying a half-breed. She is not my family, and he will never be my family."

Red Wolf seized his son's arm, gripping hard. Running Bear winced. His father had never touched him in anger before, only with affection and playfulness.

"You have much to learn," Red Wolf said. "But understand this: you will never disrespect Pale Bear or Dancing Rain. I trust Pale Bear with my life, and you should too.

Dancing Rain is as much Rain Flower's grandchild as you are. That makes her family. One day it will benefit you to have their friendship. Do not sever that tie this early in your life."

Red Wolf released Running Bear with a shove, then turned his back on him. Running Bear stood rigid. Anger burned in his chest, which was made worse by the fact that his father had disciplined him in front of his friends.

Aaron smiled when the tavern came into view. He urged his horse forward and rode into the backyard. Mary came out of the kitchen, smiling brightly.

"You're back! How was the hunt?"

"It was good," Aaron said as he dismounted. He handed her the softening deer hides. "But I let Red Wolf take all the meat. He has more mouths to feed, and deer are getting scarce around the village."

"That was good of you," Mary said. "Father has been able to buy as much as we need from the local farmers. We have more variety now, but the price of stew rose to cover our added costs."

Mary took the reins of one of the horses and followed Aaron into the barn. As soon as they were inside, Aaron bent down and kissed her. Mary wrapped her arms around his neck and kissed him back.

"I missed you," she said.

"I missed you, too, but it was good to spend time with Red Wolf," Aaron said. "He brought Running Bear along."

Mary frowned. "How did that go?"

Aaron sighed. "I'm afraid Red Wolf is going to have problems with that boy. He's very arrogant. He thought he was hiding his disdain for me, but he didn't do a good job of it."

"I'm sorry, Aaron. He would have nothing to do with me when I was at Grandmother's. I heard him whisper 'half-breed' under his breath. I pretended I didn't hear him and was nice to him." She grinned. "I think that annoyed him more than anything."

"Red Wolf asked me to teach the boy to read and write," Aaron said. "I tried. Running Bear stared at the letters and words but didn't listen and didn't care about learning."

"He will not make a good leader for the Nottoway people with that attitude," Mary said. "Red Wolf sees the wisdom in learning everything he can about the white settlers and their government. He uses his knowledge to protect his people."

"Red Wolf is a good man," Aaron said. Then he smiled. "He wants to come to the wedding."

"What wedding?" Mary asked coyly.

"Ours," Aaron said.

"I did not know we were having a wedding," Mary said innocently. "I believe it is the white man's way to ask the woman to marry him. I do not believe I have heard that question from you."

Aaron rolled his eyes. He took her hand and looked her in the eyes. "Mary, I would have you for my wife, if you are willing."

Mary smiled. "Yes. I am willing." She laughed. "Now, was that so hard?"

Aaron grinned, picked her up, and twirled her around. "Well, now that we are engaged to be married, we need to decide some very important issues. I want to buy the land in Rain Flower's vision. We must improve the land, so do you want to live there, or would you rather stay here while I improve the land and travel back and forth?"

"I will go where you go," Mary said. "Buy your land. We will travel back and forth together."

When the horses were unloaded and rubbed down, Aaron and Mary went into the kitchen. He held her hand openly. James looked at them, at their hands, then at Aaron.

Mary said, "Father, Aaron has asked me to marry him, and I have agreed."

"That so?" James asked Aaron.

"Yes, sir. We would like your blessing."

James grinned. "It's about time. Boy, you are the slowest young man I have ever seen in the romance department," he said laughing. "When do you plan to do this?"

"I want to buy the property where Red Wolf and I have been hunting," Aaron said. "It's in the mountains. The land is like a rolling hill plateau. There's a small river that goes over the side of the mountain in a waterfall. There are a variety of trees which tells me the soil will probably be good."

"The mountains you say. Southern or northern?" James asked.

"Southern mountains," Aaron said.

"You'll need to go to Brunswick Courthouse," James said. "It's about a two-day ride from here. Speak to the clerk. He'll record your claim and put you in touch with a surveyor. Take the surveyor there yourself to make sure he has the right property. Last I heard, the Crown charges five shillings for fifty acres on the patent fee. After that you pay the annual quitrent, a fancy name for property tax."

Aaron smiled. "I suppose I'd better do that. But today,

I want a bath."

Aaron gathered his clothes, soap, and a towel and went to the brewing room. When they made the whole building into the brewery, another hearth was added. Now, there was always warm water near the fire, and James had placed a tub in one corner. Aaron always looked forward to a warm bath when he returned from a hunt.

CHAPTER 17

Virginia Wilderness 1742

Aaron rode to Brunswick Courthouse wearing what he thought of as his English clothes. He was determined to buy the land, and he wanted the clerk to take him seriously.

The building sat on rock pilings. He climbed the stairs to the two room structure and stepped inside. The large front room was mostly empty, its plank flooring echoing under his boots. To the right was a smaller room where a man sat behind a desk. Behind him stood a bookshelf crowded with books, rolled maps, and boxes of papers.

Aaron stepped into the doorway.

The man looked up. "How can I help you?"

"My name is Aaron McNeil, and I would like to buy some land."

"Do you own any now?"

"No, sir," Aaron answered.

"By what right do you claim land?" the clerk asked. "When did you come to the colony?"

"I came in 1740," Aaron answered. "I paid my own passage."

"Then by headright, you may claim fifty acres." The clerk lowered his quill pen, preparing to unroll a map. "Where do you want your land? We have plenty of Brunswick County already surveyed and platted."

"The land I want is in the mountains," Aaron said.

The clerk paused, studying Aaron more closely. "The mountains? How do you know about land in the mountains?"

"I have been hunting there for two winters," Aaron said. "I know the area, and I like it."

"How did you find it?"

"My friend, Red Wolf, took me." Aaron said. "I was new then, and he took pity on me, tried to teach me the way of the wilderness."

"Did you learn?"

"I suppose so," Aaron said. "I am still alive."

The clerk huffed a quiet laugh. "You realize, do you not, that land out there is frontier. There's no protection against the Cherokee, Shawnee, or Seneca."

Aaron shrugged. "The land is a plateau surrounded by ridges. I doubt many go that way."

"Your friend Red Wolf did."

"Yes, but Red Wolf is Nottoway," Aaron said. "He came from the east. The others would come from the west or the north. I have crossed that ridge twice for salt. Salt is the only reason I would take that trail."

"You've been to the salt flats?"

"Yes, sir. Twice. My friends, James and Edward Montgomery, pay me well for whatever I can bring back."

"You are friends with the Montgomerys?" the clerk asked.

"Yes, sir. Do you know them?" Aaron asked.

"Most people in the Tidewater and Piedmont do. They ship in most of the supplies we buy." The clerk leaned back. "How much of this land do you want to buy?"

"I want to buy the whole piece, from the waterfall to the base of the western ridge," Aaron said.

"I will need to get a surveyor out there. I'm not sure I can find one who will go that far out."

"I will take the surveyor," Aaron said. "I know the way."

Just then a man in a linen shirt with buckskin breeches, leggings, moccasins, and a buckskin coat walked into the office and handed the clerk a bundle of papers.

"Jake," the clerk said, "this is Aaron McNeil. He wants to purchase land in the mountains. Would you be willing to survey it?"

Jake looked Aaron over. "Not without a guide."

"I can take you," Aaron said. "I know the parcel I want."

Jake raised an eyebrow. "You can take me?"

"Yes, sir."

A slow grin spread across Jake's face. He had no doubt the boy would be begging to go home after the first night on the trail. Well, he'd teach this youngster a lesson.

"All right. I'll go. When do you want to leave?"

"As soon as you are willing," Aaron said. "I brought provisions just in case I got lucky and found a surveyor."

"How long will it take us to get there?" Jake asked.

"We are already pretty far west," Aaron said. "If we leave now, we will spend two nights on the trail and get there the following morning. If we leave in the morning, we spend one night on the trail and arrive in the afternoon."

"Let's get some food, and leave this afternoon, then," Jake said.

Aaron smiled. "Thank you."

"Don't thank me yet," Jake said. "We still have to get there." He grinned again, already imagining the boy stumbling behind him. He led Aaron to a small tavern where they ate a bowl of stew.

Afterward, Jake said, "Give me a few minutes to get my supplies."

Aaron nodded. He took his horse and pack horse into the woods beyond the clearing. There he traded his stiff English coat and clothes for the familiar comfort of his buckskins, his hatchet and hunting knife on his belt.

Jake Webster gathered supplies from a room above the tavern. He loaded his equipment, tools, food, rifle and extra powder and shot. When he was ready, he led his horse back to the front of the courthouse. He saw the boy's horses, but not the boy.

Aaron approached him. "Mr. Webster, are you ready?"

Jake turned. The boy now wore buckskins. He almost laughed out loud. The boy certainly looked the part. Time would tell if he was the real thing or just playing at being a frontiersman.

Jake nodded. "Let's go." They mounted their horses and Jake turned to Aaron. "Which way?"

Aaron took the lead. They followed the main road until it narrowed into a forest trail. He stayed on it until almost dark, then stopped by a small stream.

"This is a good place to camp tonight."

"Have you camped here before?" Jake asked.

"I have camped by this stream but farther up the trail," Aaron said. He tethered the horses, let them drink, and built a small fire. The night was already turning cold.

He unpacked some dried venison and biscuits and

shared them with Jake. When they were finished, Aaron pulled a fur blanket from under one of the saddles and wrapped himself in it.

"Do you want the first watch or the second?"

Jake studied him. Maybe the boy was smarter than he'd thought. "I'll take the first watch."

Aaron nodded, laid down by the fire and went to sleep. Jake woke him around two in the morning. Aaron sat up instantly, turned away from the fire, and took his place on watch. Jake lay down and went to sleep.

The next morning, Jake woke to the sound of Aaron packing supplies. Aaron handed him another biscuit and some venison. After dousing the fire, they were back on the trail. Aaron rode in silence. His eyes constantly watched, and his ears listened to the forest.

At noon, Aaron stopped to water the horses and passed Jake some more food. Suddenly the horses neighed and jerked at their reins. Aaron's head snapped up. He shouldered his rifle and fired in one smooth motion.

A mountain lion crashed to the ground at Jake's feet.

Jake stared at the dead cat then at Aaron. "How did you know it was there?"

"The horses were spooked. About the only thing that makes them that scared is a mountain lion or a bear." He looked at the cat. "Do you eat those?"

Jake shook his head.

"Me neither," Aaron said. "Shame to waste the meat, but I want the fur."

With practiced skill, he skinned the animal, wiped off as much of the fat and blood as he could, and tucked the hide into the pannier. He cut the back haunches free and wrapped them in canvas.

"At least we can try it."

They were soon back on the trail.

Aaron took Jake partway up the mountain trail before stopping for the night.

"The worst is behind us," Aaron said. "The trail from here isn't as steep."

He fried the mountain lion meat. He and Jake ate it.

"It's not bad," Aaron said. "Not my favorite, but not bad."

The next morning, after a breakfast of leftover mountain lion and a biscuit, they were back on the trail.

"Don't you get tired of meat and biscuits?" Jake asked.

Aaron laughed. "Yes, but it's good traveling food. How long will it take you to survey the area?"

"I don't know," Jake said. "It depends on how big it is."

"If we camp there tonight, we can trap a rabbit. I can fry it, and I have leather britches in the pannier," Aaron said.

"Are you always this prepared on the trail?" Jake asked.

"It depends on where I'm going and why. Some trips are short and need no supplies. Others are long and need supplies that travel light,"

Aaron led his horses back onto the trail, and Jake followed. Around noon, they stopped.

"We are here," Aaron said. "This is the land I want to purchase."

Jake looked around. "Where do you want to start the property?"

Aaron smiled and led him to the top of a waterfall. "This will be one boundary."

"That's easy." Jake wrote down the information then marked the spot with a large rock. "Where next?"

Aaron led him across the top of the cliff to where the land met a mountain. "That whole area on the top of the cliff. Then from here we go southwest."

Jake and Aaron traversed the rugged terrain, marking boundaries. They had worked most of the day when Aaron suddenly whispered, "Stay still. Do not move, and whatever you do, do not raise your weapon."

Aaron put both hands in the air and walked into a small clearing. In Iroquois, he called, "I am Pale Bear, friend of the Seneca and Nottaway."

A voice answered, "Pale Bear?"

A man stepped from the trees. It was Hiawachi.

Aaron smiled. "Hiawachi it is good to see you." The men clasped hands in friendship.

"Why are you this far south?" Aaron asked.

"Hunting," Hiawachi said. "Settlers have moved all the way to the mountains to our north. Game grows scarce. We must travel farther to find meat."

Aaron nodded. "Red Wolf has the same problem. He and I hunt this area." Aaron pointed toward Jake. "He is a colony surveyor. He is taking the boundaries back to the settlement so I may buy this land. When it is mine, you will always be welcome to hunt here just as Red Wolf will be."

Hiawachi inclined his head. "Thank you, Pale Bear. This land has always had plentiful game. It has water and is protected by the ridges. You chose well."

"Come, camp with us and share our food," Aaron said.

He led Hiawachi and his men to the campsite. Aaron had trapped the promised rabbit. He served the men fried rabbit and boiled leather britches.

One of Hiawachi's companions grinned. "Pale Bear

cooks well, like a woman." The others laughed.

"I take that as a high compliment," Aaron said, smiling. "I am about to marry the daughter of Red Wolf's sister. She cooks very well."

"You are to marry a Nottoway?" Hiawachi asked.

"Mary's Nottoway name is Dancing Rain. Her father is white which is why we call her Mary."

Jake sat quietly, listening to the men talk and joke in a language he did not understand. He realized he had completely misjudged Aaron McNeil.

At last, Aaron turned to him. "Hiawachi is taking the first watch. I will take the second. You can sleep."

"You mean you trust these Indians to not kill us in our sleep?" Jake asked.

Anger surged through Aaron, but he kept his voice level. "Aye."

"Why?" Jake demanded. "They hate white men."

"Hiawachi is my friend," Aaron said. "We met two winters ago when I saved his daughter's life. He will not end mine. And he will not end yours. He knows what you are doing for me, and he wants the task completed."

"Why would he want you to own this land?" Jake asked. "That doesn't make sense."

"This area has abundant game. I told Hiawachi he may hunt here any time he wishes, just as Red Wolf does."

"Red Wolf?" Jake asked.

"Leader of the Nottoway. He is the one who showed me this place," Aaron said.

"Why would he do that?"

"I work for his brother-in-law who is white," Aaron said. "We both need meat. Get some sleep. We will be busy tomorrow."

Aaron lay down with his back to the fire. He stared into the darkness. He did not like Jake Webster very much, but he needed the man. As soon as the survey was done and the land was his, he would not have to deal with him again.

The next day they continued surveying. Their presence scared the game away, but Hiawachi and his men caught trout and packed them in salt. By the day's end, Aaron and Jake had completely covered the entire boundary.

They camped that night in the same place. Aaron again shared fried rabbit and leather britches.

"Did you pick the beans, Pale Bear?" One of the Seneca men asked. He was grinning, teasing Aaron.

Aaron shrugged. "Probably. When the three sisters give us their bounty, they do not care who picks it."

Hiawachi laughed. "Good answer, Pale Bear."

The next morning, Aaron said goodbye to his Seneca friends and led Jake down the mountain. They traveled in silence. The descent was easier, and Aaron pushed hard. He would have liked to reach the Courthouse that night, but the horses needed water and rest.

They shared venison for supper. Aaron took the second watch and woke Jake early. They were on the trail as the sky shifted from dark to gray. At midday, Aaron and Jake walked back into the Courthouse.

Aaron stood in the office while Jake calculated his measurements and wrote his report. Jake handed the final report to the clerk who read it.

"This is quite a large tract of land," the clerk said, looking at the paper. "You receive fifty acres by right and another fifty acres for paying your own passage, but the whole tract is a thousand acres." The man scribbled on a piece of paper. "Surveyor fee, quitrent, and 40 shillings per one hundred acres that would be..." his voice trailed off as he calculated the cost.

"Twenty-three sovereigns," Aaron said.

The agent blinked. "Why, you are correct," the clerk said. "Are you an educated man?"

"Aye," Aaron answered.

"Then why choose land so far away?"

"I like it," Aaron said. He lifted his shirt and took off the belt his father had given him the night he left Scotland. He ran his hand along the belt, realizing his father hadn't simply given him coin for the journey. He had given him a future. He counted out twenty-three gold coins.

"I believe that is payment for the whole tract, quitrent, and fees," Aaron said.

Jake and the clerk stared at him.

"Yes," the clerk said. "It is paid in full."

"May I have the deed?" Aaron asked.

The clerk wrote out three copies. He handed one to Aaron.

"This copy is yours," the clerk said. "I will file one here and send one to the colony land office in Williamsburg. Congratulations, Mr. McNeil, you own one thousand acres of mountain land."

Aaron took the deed, shook the clerk's hand and turned to Jake. "Thank you, Mr. Webster. You have been most helpful."

Jake hesitated. "I have to know, who are you? You're educated; you have enough money to buy that much land; you are at home in the wilderness; you are friends with the Indians, and they call you Pale Bear."

Aaron shrugged. "I am Aaron McNeil, third son of Neil McNeil, Laird of Clan McNeil in Scotland. I came here because of a threat to my life. This is my home now. What I was in Scotland matters not at all. Who I am here is what matters to me now."

He bowed. "Thank you, gentlemen."

The men watched him leave the courthouse, deed in his hand.

"He's really friends with the Indians?" the clerk asked.

"Yes," Jake said. "And he saved my life when a mountain lion leapt out of tree toward me. I do not think we have heard the last of Aaron McNeil."

CHAPTER 18

Norfolk, Virginia 1742

Aaron rode into the backyard of the tavern, dust rising from the horses' hooves. Gordon came up to him and held the reins while Aaron dismounted.

"Did you get your land?"

"Aye," Aaron said grinning. "It's bigger than I expected, a full thousand acres."

Gordon let out a low whistle. "Congratulations, but I do not envy you the task of taming the wilderness and improving it. I'm happy here in town."

Aaron laughed and headed inside. In the kitchen, Mary heard the door open. She turned, squealed and ran to him. He caught her up and swung her around. James appeared in the doorway, smiling when he saw who had caused the commotion.

"Well?" James asked.

Aaron held up a folded paper. "I own a thousand acres in the mountains. I've three years to improve it."

James's eyes warmed. "A thousand acres. That's no small thing. Well done. When do you plan to go?"

"I thought to leave after we've planted the gardens here," Aaron said. "The place won't support us for a while. I'll be lucky to get a cabin and barn raised by fall. Then maybe next spring Mary and I can move there."

"Tell us about it," Mary said, her eyes bright.

"The land is an odd shape, like a many-sided box, which made the surveying slow. The eastern edge begins at a cliff. A stream rises on the steep mountain to the west, runs through the property and spills over the cliff in a waterfall. The stream is clear as glass and cold enough to numb your hands. There are trout in it. The woods are thick with all sorts of trees, and I think apple trees would take well. There's one open meadow, and the view of the mountains from it is magnificent."

He paused, picturing it again.

"I plan to farm the end of the property nearest the waterfall. I'll leave the western side wild for now. It's full of game. Red Wolf will need to get meat for his village. Hiawachi of the Seneca wants to hunt there as well. He says the settlers are pressing closer, and game is growing scarce. He may have to move his whole village to survive."

"I'm not surprised," James said. "Ships come in every day with immigrants, and that's just in Norfolk. Add the other ports, and the wave of people must be overwhelming to the natives."

Aaron stretched and smiled. "I need a bath."

Mary handed him a bar of soap and a towel. He fetched his English clothes from the pannier and walked to the brewing house. Soon he was sinking into the hot water, scrubbing the dirt from his skin. He leaned his head back and stared at the ceiling, a slow smile spreading across his face.

He owned one thousand acres. That was more than the McNeil holding on the mainland. His father would be proud. That belt of gold coins had not just kept him safe on the journey, it had given him a future.

The days passed as Aaron and Mary made plans for moving to the mountains.

"Mary, I'm going to build a bed frame long enough and wide enough for me to be comfortable. I'm thinking seven feet long and six feet wide. Can you make a mattress that size?"

"Yes. I'll start working on the linens in my spare time," she said.

Aaron looked doubtful. "We'll never get linens. You never have spare time."

Mary laughed. "I'll make time, silly."

Aaron grinned.

In early March, Gordon came to Aaron. "I'm going to the docks."

"Why?" he asked.

"I watch the ships to see if any of our clan are on them," Gordon said. "I remember how frightened I was. I want to help anyone from Clan McNeil."

"I'll go with you," Aaron said.

"Better bring money."

"Why?"

"Some of them are sold as indentured servants to the highest bidder," Gordon said.

Aaron stopped short. Stunned. "I had no idea!"

"Come on," Gordon said. "A ship just docked."

Aaron and Gordon walked down the hill to the wharf.

Sailors were lowering gangplanks and shouting orders as passengers prepared to disembark. On this ship, the crew gathered passengers to one side of the dock, separating them from the watching crowd.

The captain stood on the deck, projecting his voice over the noise. "These people are to be servants. If you pay their passage, they will work for you for seven years."

Gordon scanned the line of weary faces. Suddenly, he punched Aaron lightly on the arm.

"Look there," he said. "It's Evan Fletcher! What's he doing on that boat? He transports whiskey into England for your uncle."

"He must've been caught," Aaron said. "Who is that holding on to him?"

"I don't know her," Gordon said. "But they're clinging to each other. They should be sold as a pair, but they likely won't be."

Aaron pushed through the crowd and approached the first mate standing on the wharf.

"Yes?" the man asked.

"How much for that man and that woman?" Aaron asked, pointing to Evan and the girl.

The mate named the price. Aaron counted out the coins without hesitation. The man nodded, walked over to the pair, and told them to follow the tall, blond gentleman.

Aaron watched them approach. The woman was trembling, her eyes red from crying. Evan looked thin and hollow-eyed. The voyage had clearly been hard.

When they got closer, Aaron said softly, "Evan Fletcher?"

Evan blinked in confusion.

Aaron held out his hand. "Aaron McNeil."

Shock flickered across Evan's face. He grasped Aaron's hand.

"Are you the Laird's boy that disappeared?"

"Aye. Father sent me here," Aaron said. "My life was in danger from my own brother."

"He's gone," Evan said. "Your brother, John. He ran off to Rome to help James Stuart regain the throne. Duncan is helping the Laird, now."

Aaron shook his head, "I hope John finds what he is looking for. Who is your lady?"

"This is Molly Brewster."

"Hello, Molly," Aaron said. "You're safe now." He gestured toward the town. "Come on. Let's get some food in you."

They followed him up the wharf. Gordon met them halfway.

"Hello, Evan," Gordon said.

Evan stared. "Gordon McNeil?"

"Aye," Gordon said with a grin. "Blair and I came over last year. It's a good place, Evan."

Aaron led Evan and Molly to the Running Hare. Inside, he found James behind the counter.

"James, this is Evan Fletcher and Molly Brewster. I bought their passage, so I suppose they're part of the family for the next seven years. Evan is McNeil clan."

James nodded at the couple. "Welcome." He turned to Aaron. "She'll have to room with Mary, and he can room with you. The other rooms are full of people waiting for passage back to England."

Aaron nodded and turned back to Evan and Molly. "Do you have any bags?"

Both shook their heads.

"What happened?" Aaron asked gently.

Evan sighed. "I was caught taking whiskey into England. They offered me prison in England or transportation. I chose Virginia. Molly was accused of stealing food at the market. She tried to tell them she wasn't stealing, but they wouldn't hear it. She chose transportation, too. We were chained in the same prison wagon that carried us to the dock. We've been watching out for each other since."

Mary entered with two small bowls of stew and tankards of water. She set them before the newcomers.

"Eat small and slow," Aaron said. "Otherwise, you'll be sick. You look better than I did when I got off the boat."

"I will agree with that," James said. "My nephew, Edward, was the first mate. He brought Aaron up here, and he was just a skinny thing. He's grown inches and muscles since then."

"Aye," Evan said. "I didn't recognize you."

When they were finished eating, Aaron said, "No offense, but you need a bath and clean clothes."

"No offense taken," Evan said. "I agree, but I've nothing else to wear."

"You're not much shorter than I am, you can wear mine until yours are clean," Aaron said.

Mary smiled at Molly. "You can wear some of my clothes. Come with me. Ladies first."

Mary helped Molly fill the tub with hot water, and gave her soap, a towel, and a clean skirt and blouse. She set more water over the fire to warm for Evan.

When Molly finished, Aaron showed Evan where everything was. Returning to the kitchen, he found Molly sitting at the table peeling potatoes. Her hair was wet, but she looked calmer, almost relieved.

Aaron filled the wash pot with water and set it over a fire outside. When the water boiled, he dropped Evan and Molly's clothes in to boil away any disease or lice. When it cooled enough, he let Molly wash them with soap.

That evening, Blair and Molly were cooking the food and serving the patrons in the dining room. Mary went to her room. Her spinning wheel and loom sat in the corner. She started spinning the combed cotton, the small fibers twisting into a light beige thread. She imagined the linens she would weave from it. They would be smooth, sturdy, and hers.

Aaron came into the kitchen and looked around. "Where's Mary?"

"In her room," Blair said.

Aaron walked to the open door of Mary's room. He looked in and was surprised to see the weaving equipment.

"I did not know this was in here."

"And why would you?" Mary asked without looking up. "You would never be allowed to enter my room."

"So, this is how you make the linens," he said.

Mary smiled. "Yes, and when we move, these are going with me. Make the cabin big enough for your bed, my weaving tools, and a table with chairs. Shelves and hooks on the walls would be good, too."

Aaron chuckled. "Already demanding things and we are not yet wed. Well, I can live with that as long as you demand kisses, too."

Mary batted her eyes. "Oh, I will always demand those."

By the middle of March, the planting behind the tavern was almost completed. Aaron approached Evan.

"I am going to the mountains, and I need you to help me. Will you be agreeable?"

"Of course," Evan said then grinned. "I'm tied to you for seven years."

Aaron frowned. "Let's not dwell on that. I am glad I was able to help a clansman. If a good opportunity opens for you, we can discuss that. I would not want to hold you back."

Evan's expression softened. "Seeing the mountains seems like a good opportunity to me. When do we leave?"

"As soon as James's crops are in the ground," Aaron said.

Two days later, Aaron drove a wagon being pulled by two draft horses into the barnyard behind the tavern.

Evan walked over. "Those are good looking horses, Aaron."

In the back of the wagon lay saws, spades, hammers, axes, adzes, wedges, nails, and other assorted tools. There were two of everything. There were pots and pans, rope, chains, picks, a plow, and a harrow. At the bottom sat a box with ladles, wooden trenchers, bowls, and spoons. There was a large fork for handling meat, and two pewter forks for eating rested on top.

"You're definitely prepared," Evan said.

Aaron pulled the wagon under some trees and covered it with two rolls of canvas.

"I hope I have what we need. It will be hard work, but two can do it easily." He looked at Evan. "The trip will be slow. In some places we will have to widen the trail for the wagon, but once that is done, traveling back and forth will be easier."

The next morning, Aaron and Evan were prepared to leave just as the sun was rising. Mary held on to Aaron tightly, her cheek pressed to his chest.

"Please be careful," she said.

"I will," Aaron said smiling. "I have Evan to protect me from myself and my crazy ways."

"Humpf," Mary said. "Crazy is putting it mildly."

Aaron laughed, but when he pulled back, he saw the worry in Mary's eyes. He brushed a strand of hair from her face and whispered, "I'll come back to you."

James shook Aaron's hand. "Take care. I'll expect you both back for the harvest."

Aaron and Evan waved as they drove the wagon to the road. Their horses were tethered to the back. They crossed the river on the ferry and began making their way west.

CHAPTER 19

Appalachian Mountains, Virginia 1742

The first few days of the journey went smoothly, though the road was rutted from the winter rains. Aaron told Evan about how much farther west the good roads reached now than when he first went to the mountains. But once the main roads ended, progress slowed. They stopped often to remove a fallen tree or cut away briars and vines.

A week into the journey, the men were clearing another fallen log from the wilderness path when the sky began to darken. By late afternoon, thunder rolled across the hills.

"We should stop early," Aaron said.

He found a stand of oak trees with small but substantial leaves. They barely had enough time to pull the wagon under them before the storm broke. Evan and Aaron tethered the horses to the trees. Already soaked, they climbed into the wagon under the canvas.

Rain hammered the canvas. The wind snapped the material like a sail, and rain blew in under it, soaking the men again and again. The water ran in rivulets under the wheels, and the horses stamped nervously.

Evan shouted over the roar. "This is a fine night!"

Aaron laughed despite the cold rain running down his neck. "Aye. A fine night to test our spirits."

Lightning split the sky, illuminating the forest in stark white for an instant. From under the canvas, Aaron could see the trees bending in the wind like reeds, proof of the storm's raw force. The tempest raged for hours. Their firewood was soaked, their blankets damp, and neither man slept more than a few minutes at a time. By dawn, the storm had passed, leaving the world washed clean and glistening.

Evan groaned as he climbed down from the wagon. "I think that storm beat me more than the work will."

Aaron stretched his stiff back. "We'll be sore today, but we'll dry out soon enough."

After three weeks of slow, steady travel, they arrived. Aaron stopped the wagon in a small clearing and un-hitched the horses.

"This is it," he said quietly.

Evan looked around, taking in the towering pines and the gentle slope of the land.

Aaron stood still for a long moment, letting the sight settle into him. This was the place he had thought about for years. Wild, quiet, and full of promise.

"Let's set up camp," Aaron said. "Then I will show you where I want to put the cabin."

They used part of the canvas for shelter, reinforcing it with limbs and pine boughs. Aaron led Evan a short way into the woods.

"Here," Aaron said. "The door will face south."

Evan turned southward and saw where the land began to slope downward. "You'll have a good view once this is cleared."

"That's the plan," Aaron said, picking up an axe. "No better time to start than right now."

By evening, two tall pines lay felled and debarked. Aaron wiped sweat from his brow.

"I feel good about today," he said. "I hope I feel as good tomorrow."

Evan stretched his aching arms. "I think I'm going to be sore tomorrow."

Aaron grinned. "Probably. I will be too."

When they had cleared an acre of land, Aaron used the horses and plow to cut the outline of the cabin he envisioned. The horses snorted softly in the warm air as the soil turned dark and rich beneath the blade. He and Evan cleared the building site and leveled the ground just enough to set the foundation stones.

As Evan and Aaron continued to clear the land, they hauled the stones they pried from the earth to the cabin site. They stacked them into short pilings. Broad flat stones sat on the bottom and smaller ones on the top, which raised the cabin a foot above the ground. When the pilings were level and steady, they laid heavy oak sill logs across them, the squared timbers forming the base of the structure.

Oak floor joists were notched, fitted onto the sills, and secured with nails. Aaron and Evan sawed pine boards, dried them in the sun, then planed them smooth. The scent of sap clung to their hands for days. They nailed the boards across the joists, creating a solid raised floor with cool air circulating beneath it to keep the cabin dry.

With the foundation secure, they began stacking the wall logs, fitting each notch with practiced rhythm. As the walls rose, the stones they had gathered were shaped into two chimneys. One hearth was large with a hinged cooking hook and a stone oven. The other was smaller, meant only for heat.

With the walls in place, Evan and Aaron cut the ridge-pole and rafters. After one long, back-breaking day, the skeleton of the roof was finished, ready for the shingles. The next day, they began splitting shingles, using straight-grained pine and oak. The steady sound of the mallet and the scent of fresh wood filled the clearing as piles of shingles grew at their feet.

When they had enough, they climbed onto the rafters and began laying the shingles in overlapping rows, starting at the eaves and working upward. The roof took shape slowly, row by row.

By the time they finished, the sun was low and the air smelled of pine, oak, and sweat. Aaron climbed down the ladder and stood back, hands on his hips.

"That will keep the rain out," he said with pride.

"Aye," Evan said. "It looks like a real home now."

Two months after arriving, Aaron and Evan stepped into the finished cabin. Shutters opened to let in light and air. The doors swung on their strap hinges and locked from the inside. The back area had a hearth, a large oversized bed frame, and enough room for Mary's weaving equipment. Aaron stood in the middle of the cabin, looked around and let out a long breath of satisfaction.

They broke camp and moved into the cabin that night. Their next project was a barn. By late August, the cabin, a barn, a spring house over a small creek, and an outhouse down the hill were all completed. Five acres of land had been cleared. Chopped wood was stacked in the barn, and the area around the homestead had been planted in red clover from England, the tiny leaves already beginning to sprout.

Aaron sat heavily on a bench in front of the cabin. "I am tired," he groaned. "I want to sleep in a real bed for at least a whole day."

Evan nodded, too worn out to speak.

"Thank you," Aaron said quietly. "By myself, I'd barely have the cabin finished. Let's cool off in the creek and pack the wagon. We're going back to Norfolk tomorrow. James should be about ready to harvest his crops."

Aaron stripped down to his loincloth and lay in the creek, letting the cold water run over his hot, tired muscles. Evan followed, sighing as the chill eased the soreness in his back. Over the summer, Aaron had taught him how to preserve deer hides and make buckskins. Evan now had moccasins, a loincloth with a skirt, and leggings, all worn with his linen shirt. Eventually, he'd have enough hides for a buckskin shirt of his own. But most days, the men worked in just their moccasins, leggings, loincloth, and skirt. It was too hot for shirts.

The sky had barely turned from gray to blue when Aaron and Evan started the trip back to Norfolk. Aaron slowed the horses and stopped at the cave.

"Why are we stopping?" Evan asked. "We just got started."

Aaron grinned. He took a stick and parted the vines, then wrapped them around nearby branches.

"Careful of the vines," Aaron said. "Poison ivy."

Evan blinked. "That's a cave!"

"Glad you noticed," Aaron said, laughing. "Come inside."

Aaron checked the floor and saw no prints from when he and Red Wolf had swept it clean several months before. Evan followed him into the cool, dim space behind the waterfall. The air smelled of damp stone and old earth. Aaron lit a small fire for light, and together they carried the tools into the small room where the bear had once slept.

"Next trip up, we can bring other things," Aaron said as they restarted their journey. "Mary wants shelves, hooks, seeds, pottery, and her weaving equipment."

"That cave is part of the reason you wanted this place, isn't it?" Evan said.

"Yes. Red Wolf and I spent two winters here, hunting and trapping."

"Red Wolf?" Evan asked.

"Mary's uncle. Her mother's brother from the Nottoway tribe. He's a good man. He taught me how to survive in this land. You'll meet him at the wedding."

The path they had cleared on their way to the mountains made their return to Norfolk much easier. They were only a day from town when Aaron and Evan made their usual midday stop to rest the horses and let them drink. As they ate dried venison, Aaron suddenly motioned for silence. He eased their rifles out of the wagon, handed Evan his, and slipped into the woods.

Two men rode up a few minutes later. They stopped, got off their horses and began rummaging through the back of the wagon and the panniers on the horses.

"Cover me," Aaron whispered.

He stepped into the clearing. "Excuse me, but I'd rather you not steal my belongings."

The men jumped. One pulled his pistol. "I don't think you have a say in the matter." He strode toward Aaron. "I think I'll take that knife of yours, too."

"No," Aaron said calmly. "I'd like to keep that."

The man cocked the pistol. "Have it your way."

Before the man could fire, Aaron lunged, seized the pistol, and drove the hatchet into the man's throat in one swift, brutal motion. The second man raised his rifle, but Aaron fired the pistol first. The shot echoed through the trees.

Aaron stared at the bodies, sadness settling over him like a weight. Evan approached, pale and shaken.

"All they had to do was keep going," Aaron murmured. "I would have given them food if they would have just kept moving."

"Where did you learn to do that?" Evan asked.

Aaron shrugged. "Sometimes you don't think, you just react. And you must react quickly or die. This is a harsh land."

Aaron stripped the men of valuables and weapons. They tethered the horses to the wagon and continued their journey to Norfolk.

James was coming out of the brewing room when Aaron drove the wagon into the barnyard. He saw the extra horses and felt his stomach sink. He knew Aaron hated killing, even in self defense.

James approached the wagon. "Are you hurt?"

"No," Aaron said, shaking his head. "Just disgusted."

James looked at Evan. "Are you alright?"

Evan swallowed. "Yes."

Mary came running out of the house, joy lighting her face, until she saw the horses and Aaron's expression. She slowed and raised her hand to her mouth.

"Oh," she whispered. She stepped close and touched his cheek. "How are you?"

He wrapped his arms around her. "Better now. You have a cabin, a barn, a spring house, and an outhouse. And several acres planted in clover."

Mary stepped back, stunned. "All that? You must be exhausted. Come into the kitchen as soon as you see to the horses. I'll have a meal ready for you."

When Aaron took the horses to the barn, James placed a hand on Evan's shoulder. "What's wrong?"

Evan shook his head. "I've never seen anything like what happened. In less than a minute, they were both dead. He's... he's lethal. I don't know whether to be frightened or glad he is my friend!"

"Don't be frightened," James said. "Aaron is gentle unless he or someone he cares about is threatened. He was protecting you as much as defending himself."

"I know," Evan said quietly. "But he's the Laird's son. I should have been protecting him."

James smiled. "That means nothing here. Forget those old ways. Here you can be as successful as any Laird. If you keep thinking of others as your betters, you'll never rise above what you were in Scotland. It's hard to change your thinking when you're indentured, but think of this time as a chance to learn, not servitude. You can learn a lot from Aaron."

"Aye," Evan said. "You're right."

Aaron sat at the kitchen table eating mutton, potatoes and wilted greens.

"Tell me about the cabin," Mary said.

Aaron smiled. "It faces south and has the most glorious view of the mountains. The creek runs along the side of it. There's fresh water and a spring house to keep milk and butter cool in the summer. The barn is behind and to the left. Three stalls on each side. The outhouse is downhill from the cabin. Everywhere we cleared land, I planted clover to feed cattle and keep the soil from washing away."

"What else?" Mary asked.

"You have a large hearth with your hook on a hinge, but there's no furniture except the bed frame. The cabin is a rectangle. I put a second hearth at the opposite end. I'm hoping the two fires will keep us warm."

"It sounds wonderful," Mary said softly. "I'm sad we cannot live there now."

"Spring," Aaron said. "We'll take our seeds and go in the spring. That gives me time to make some furniture this winter." Aaron grinned. "And your shelves."

Mary laughed. "Yes, you'd better."

A few days later, the harvest began. With fresh grain, Aaron returned to brewing and filling the bottles James had managed to acquire.

CHAPTER 20

Scottish Hebrides 1743

Fletcher McNeil handed his horse over to the groom. The ride back from town had been bitter, and snow had begun to fall. He stepped into the kitchen and stood by the hearth, letting the heat soak into his bones. He was getting old. There was a time when he would have come in from the cold and gone straight to work. Now, he spent more time warming his stiff joints than doing the work he once took pride in.

After shrugging off his overcoat, Fletcher walked into the small sitting room, the one that was easiest to heat. His brother and their friend were talking.

"You're back!" Ian said. "I'm glad you made it before the snow worsened."

"I'm glad you're back, and I'm glad I'm here," Neil said. "I would rather weather the storm with friends than in that drafty castle on the island."

Fletcher smiled. "Company does make things better." He handed a letter to Ian. "This was waiting for you in town."

Ian's face brightened. His daughter, Megan, had written. He opened the letter and looked at the date.

"This was written late last summer," he said. "It has taken five months to get here. That's not too shabby for having to come across the ocean and then all of England and Scotland."

"What does she say?" Neil asked. "Any word of Aaron?"

Ian read the letter aloud.

"Dear Father, I have much news. First, I have remarried."

Ian looked at his friends and smiled. "I'm happy for her."

"Go on!" Neil urged.

Ian continued.

"His name is Edward Montgomery, and yes, he is English, but none of that matters here. He and his uncle, James Montgomery, own two ships, a wharf, a general store, a warehouse, and a tavern with rooms to rent. They are quite successful. When I first got here, I worked in the tavern which is where I met Edward. Now I help Edward in the store."

"Father, can you tell Fletcher McNeil that Evan Fletcher is here, safe and sound. He was taken by the English and transported. Aaron bought his indenture, and he will work here for seven years. I have no doubt that Aaron will not hold him to the full contract. Aaron is very generous."

Fletcher let out a slow breath of relief.

Ian read on.

"Please tell the Laird that Aaron is quite successful. He owns one thousand acres of land in the mountains of Virginia. He is engaged to be married to James's daughter, Mary, and has made quite a reputation for himself. He is altogether fearsome when he puts on his buckskin clothes, a hunting knife and hatchet at his belt, and his rifle draped over his arm. He speaks one of the Indian languages and is known to be friends with two different tribes. The Indians call him Pale Bear because he is blond. He taught Mary and her uncle, Red Wolf, to read and write. If I could tell Laird McNeil anything, I would tell him he should be proud of Aaron who is both a gentleman and a warrior in every sense of the words."

Ian looked up. Neil was smiling broadly.

"Finally, Father, Edward's ships are *Tidewater Queen* and *Virginia Spirit*. If you wish to come to Virginia, either of those ships will bring you right to us in Norfolk. We would love for you to come live with us. Michael and Emmy are growing so fast, you won't want to miss their childhood. Start a passage in March. Usually, one of the ships winters in London and sets sail in late February or by March 1. Both captains have your name and will give you accommodations with the crew. Please think about coming. If you get to Norfolk, find the Running Hare Tavern, have a meal, and send for us. All my love, Megan."

When Ian finished reading, the men fell quiet at the news.

"Well," Ian said at last. "I may think about going to Virginia. It would be good to be with Megan and the children when I am old, well even older than I am now." He hesitated and looked at Neil. "I'm sorry to say this, but ever since John came to my cottage, my heart has not been here, and I cannot work like I once did."

"No, Ian," Neil said. "It is I who am sorry. If you wish to go to Virginia, I will pay your way to London, and for a room until one of those ships is ready to sail. I owe you that." He paused. "I would miss you, my friend, but I think going would be good for you. And accommodations with the crew will be far better than in the hull with the other immigrants."

Ian nodded slowly. "I believe I want to go to Virginia."

Neil thought for a moment. "I was planning on sending a ship to London with wool yarn to sell. I will do that in time to get you there by mid February. Will you take a letter to Aaron for me?"

"Of course," Ian said.

Fletcher spoke up. "Will you take Evan Fletcher's younger brother as well? I am responsible for those boys, and I let one get arrested. Virginia is a place they can make something of themselves."

Ian smiled. "It will be good to have the company. Send him with me. How old is the boy now? Thirteen? Fourteen?"

"Fourteen," Fletcher said. "I want him out of Scotland before he gets recruited to fight with the Jacobites. It's just a matter of time before James or his son are here with an army."

Neil had his men gather the wool cloth and spun yarn. When the ship was loaded, Ian McNeil and young Jamie Fletcher boarded to begin their long voyage to Virginia.

Ian shook Neil's hand. "Thank you, Neil. I will get this letter to Aaron and tell him that you are proud of him. Every son needs to hear that from his father."

Fletcher pulled Jamie to the side. "Stay with Ian. He will get you to Norfolk and to your brother." He lowered his voice. "Don't let anyone know about the coin I gave you to share with Evan. And look out for Ian. He is old and will sleep a lot. He will look like an easy target to thieves."

Jamie nodded. "I understand. I'll get him to the Running Hare in Norfolk safe. You can count on me."

"I know, lad," Fletcher said. "I've always known you could be trusted. Make me proud and make yourself a good life in Virginia. Remember, pay Aaron for Evan's indenture so he will be free. And Jamie, remember to help anyone from the clan who shows up alone and afraid as Aaron helped Evan."

"I will." Jamie smiled and boarded the ship. He was excited, and not at all afraid.

Neil McNeil's merchant vessel docked in London in mid February. Ian and Jamie disembarked and started to look for one of the ships belonging to Megan's husband. Moored at one of the larger docks was the *Virginia Spirit.*

Ian approached the gangplank and asked to speak with the captain. Captain Ivers came down to meet him.

"My name is Ian McNeil," Ian said. "I was told to see you for passage to Virginia. My daughter is Megan Montgomery."

Captain Ivers shook Ian's hand warmly. "Mr. McNeil, your daughter will be beside herself with joy when she sees you arriving in Norfolk. Bring your things aboard. We're loading cargo now and will sail with the tide in a few days."

"This is my companion, Jamie Fletcher," Ian said. "I hope it's not too much to ask if there is room for him to stay with me."

"Of course, he can," the captain said. "I'll show you where you'll stay."

Ian and Jamie settled into the crew quarters assigned to them. They had a hammock and a wool blanket.

"I'm glad we brought an extra blanket with us," Ian said. "It's still quite chilly, but I'm sure it will warm up as we cross the ocean. I've been told Virginia is very warm."

"We will be fine, Mr. McNeil," Jamie said.

"Jamie, call me Ian. We're going to be good friends by the time we get off this boat," Ian said with a smile.

Two days later, the *Virginia Spirit* sailed with the morning tide. Ian and Jamie stood at the rail and watched London and the English countryside pass by. At last, the open sea spread before them.

Jamie grinned. "This is it, Ian. We are on our way."

Chapter 21

Norfolk, Virginia 1743

The tavern was closed. Megan, Mary, Blair and Molly had filled the dining area with all the spring flowers they could gather. Now, they were in Mary's room helping her get ready for her wedding.

Megan had managed to get some blue silk and muslin and had sewn Mary a new dress. Mary's hair was pulled back and threaded with tiny blossoms. Blair had fashioned Mary a bouquet to carry into the room.

Aaron, dressed in his best English clothes, waited in the dining room with the other men and the priest from the Church of England.

At noon, the kitchen door opened, and Mary walked in holding James's arm. Her smile was so bright her cheeks ached, but she didn't care. For a heartbeat, she felt the room blur with flowers, faces, and the aroma of food. Then she saw Aaron.

Aaron's heart fluttered. Mary was beautiful, radiant. He smiled, took her hand and turned toward the priest. Five minutes later, vows were spoken, and they were husband

and wife. Aaron kissed his bride.

James hugged Mary tightly. "Be happy, daughter, and don't forget to come visiting. I love you."

"I love you, too, Father," Mary said. "Have Red Wolf bring you to the cabin when he goes hunting."

Red Wolf hugged Mary. "You have chosen your husband well, Dancing Rain. Be happy."

"I will. Thank you for coming," Mary said.

The newlyweds sat at the head of the table while everyone else found seats. Molly and Blair served the meal then joined the group. Laughter and conversation filled the room. A movement at the window caught Gordon's eye.

He stood abruptly. "That's Ian McNeil!"

Megan spun around, saw her father, and ran to the door.

"I can't believe you came!" she exclaimed and threw herself into Ian's arms, tears spilling down her cheeks. She pulled Ian inside and over to Edward.

"Edward, this is my father, Ian McNeil."

Edward smiled. "Welcome to Virginia, sir. You have made Megan the second happiest woman in Norfolk today."

"Who's the happiest?" Ian asked.

"I am," Mary said. "I am Mary Montgomery McNeil. I just married Aaron."

Ian looked around, confused. Aaron laughed, stood and extended his hand.

"Ian, I'm Aaron."

Ian blinked, startled. "I didn't recognize you!" He looked Aaron over again. He saw broader shoulders, sun-darkened skin, and the quiet confidence of a man who had carved a life out of the wilderness.

"You've... changed," Ian said.

Aaron laughed. "Aye. Virginia will do that to a man."

"I brought Jamie Fletcher with me," Ian added.

Evan had already found Jamie and was hugging his brother.

"How did you get here?" Evan asked.

"Fletcher sent me," Jamie said. "He feels bad he let you get arrested and transported. He sent me to be with you because he thinks we'll have a better life here than in Scotland."

"He's right," Evan said. "This is a good place."

James added two more chairs and plates.

"Everybody, eat before the food gets cold."

After the meal, Mary served slices of her wedding cake, which was covered with a generous icing of butter, sugar, and milk. Such a rich sweet was rare, and everyone savored it.

When the dining room was cleaned, James opened the door for business. A ship had come in and the room would be full that night.

Megan and Edward were preparing to leave. Before Ian joined them, he handed Aaron a letter.

"Your father sent this," he said. "Megan has been writing to me about everything you've done. How you helped her, Gordon, Blair and Evan. About all your accomplishments. She asked that I tell the Laird. Aaron, your father is very proud of you. Part of him wishes he could have come to Virginia with me, but he has responsibilities that will never allow it. He misses you, Aaron, but he is proud." Ian clapped Aaron on the shoulder then left with his daughter's family.

Ian went home with Megan and her family. Mary moved into Aaron's room for the short amount of time they had left in Norfolk. Jamie and Evan took a spare room upstairs, and Molly remained in Mary's old room. James sighed; life was changing. At least he still had Gordon, Blair, Molly, Evan, and Jamie.

The next day Jamie approached Aaron with the money Fletcher had given him.

"Aaron," Jamie said, "Fletcher wanted me to repay you for buying Evan's indenture. He was grateful you had done that instead of a stranger."

Aaron smiled. "Keep it for you and Evan. Evan more than earned his wages last summer at my homestead."

Aaron motioned Evan and Molly over and seated them at the table. He looked at both of them.

"Consider yourselves free of your indenture," Aaron said. "Your hard work over the past year has more than paid for your passage. I don't know what your plans will be, but stay here and help James until you decide. You're safe here." Then he stood and stepped out the kitchen door, leaving the three young people staring at each other, stunned at Aaron's generosity.

The brewing room was empty. Aaron sat down by the fire and took out the letter from his father. He had not had any time the day before to read it. He broke the seal and began to read.

January 1743. Dear Aaron. If you are reading this, I know Ian made it to Virginia safely. Megan has written him about everything that has happened to her, to you, and to the other members of our clan who have gone to Virginia. She credits you with their health, safety, and good fortunes. Megan told him about your purchase of land and how you have become a frontiersman. It all sounds exciting, but it also sounds like a lot of hard work and danger. I knew you could succeed there, but I had no idea at just how successful you would be. Aaron, I am very proud of the man you have become. Since Megan's letter, the stories of your exploits and generosity have been told to many here, and you are becoming famous in our corner of the world.

I want to tell you that John has gone to Rome to help restore James Stuart to the throne. Rumors abound that they will bring an army to Scotland. If that happens, I don't know what will happen to the McNeil clan. Our fortunes will depend on who wins the conflict. It is possible that Duncan and I may have to flee to Virginia. As much as I would like to do that and see you, I must think about our people here. If the conflict is lost and John must flee, he knows where you are. John has grown evil. If he should come to Virginia, protect yourself and your family at all costs. Do not trust him to honor familial connections.

Now, the hour grows late, and I must get this letter to Ian who has promised to put it in your hands himself. While I miss you, I do not regret sending you to Virginia. You have my utmost respect. With loving affection, Neil MacNeil.

Aaron blinked back the tears. His father was a good man, bound by duty, but he was proud, truly proud of the son he had sent across the ocean. The ache Aaron had carried for years, wondering what his father thought, began to ease.

Smiling, Aaron refolded the letter. He would place it in the box with the other letter and the McNeil ring. A re-newed sense of purpose filled him, and he began loading the wagon. He and Mary would leave in the morning.

The sun was turning the sky pink. James shook Aaron's hand and hugged Mary tightly.

"Come back and visit," he said. "Starting a homestead is hard. Work hard, but if you need to winter here for a year or two, you're welcome."

"Thank you, James," Aaron said. "We may be doing that." He helped Mary onto the wagon seat, then climbed up beside her. They waved goodbye as he guided the heavily loaded wagon out of the yard. Two horses were tethered to the back of the wagon, their panniers full of supplies.

Mary's tears flowed freely down her cheeks. Aaron reached over and squeezed her hand.

"I know it's hard," he said. "I feel it, too, but I think we'll see them this fall. We'll likely winter here. That's why I didn't buy a cow. There is too little land cleared to grow enough food this summer to tide us over to next year. We're fortunate to have your father's tavern to return to."

Mary nodded and wiped her cheeks. "I know. I've lived there my whole life. I'm indulging in a sentimental moment, that's all. I'm excited to see our new home."

Aaron squeezed her hand again. "Me too."

CHAPTER 22

Appalachian Mountains, Virginia 1743

"We're almost there," Aaron said. A burst of energy pushed through the weariness of the long journey.

Beside him, Mary leaned forward, trying to take in everything at once. The narrow path wound through a dense forest. The canopy of branches interlaced so tightly overhead the sky appeared only in scattered fragments.

Aaron slowed the wagon and smiled. "Mrs. McNeil," he said with a playful nod of his head and a grand sweep of his arm, "may I present your new home."

The wagon rolled into the clearing and stopped.

Mary stared at the cabin, the barn, and the spring house that straddled the stream. The outhouse sat hidden by the cabin.

"Oh, my," she whispered. "Aaron, you did a wonderful job."

"Well, Evan helped," he said grinning. A flicker of relief crossed his face. He hadn't realized how much he wanted her approval until that moment.

"I want to see the inside," she said, already trying to climb down.

"Hold on." Aaron hopped down and reached for her. "I'll help you. I don't want you tripping over your skirt and getting hurt your first day here." His hands settled on her waist as he lifted her down.

Mary gathered her skirt and went running to the front porch of the cabin. She stood there and looked at the view.

"I'm so glad you faced the cabin this way," she said. "It's perfect."

Aaron opened the door. "Wait."

Mary stopped, puzzled.

Aaron swept her up and carried her into the cabin. "I hear that's good luck."

She laughed softly as he set her down. Turning in a slow circle, she took in the large kitchen hearth with its hinged hook and stone oven.

"It's perfect," she said. At the far end of the cabin, she spotted the smaller hearth. "Two hearths?"

"The stone was here," Aaron said with a shrug. "I had to do something with it when we were clearing the land."

Mary's eyes sparked. "There's your overly large bed-frame. I'm glad I finished that mattress that's taking up half the wagon."

A narrow set of steps led upward. Mary climbed them and peered into the loft. "This is a very nice loft." She looked down and grinned. "Children could have a good time up here."

Aaron rubbed the back of his neck nervously. "The cabin is one long room now, but I thought... someday... we may want to section off a bedroom. That's why I added the second hearth. I just thought..." His voice trailed off in an uncharacteristic lack of confidence.

Mary stepped close and took his hands.

"It's perfect," she said softly. "You thought wonderfully."

Mary opened the back door and stepped onto the porch. Aaron brought out one of the benches he had stored inside.

"There are benches for the front porch, too," he said.

"Let's see the barn." Mary left the porch and crossed the grass. When Aaron opened the doors, she gasped. The interior was larger than it appeared from the outside, with three stalls on each side.

"I'll probably use the very back stall for hay, tack, and tools," Aaron said. "I didn't take time to build a tool shed."

Mary stepped beneath the porch-like overhang on the right side. "You can just pull the wagon through and unhitch the horses! The wagon stays dry. Aaron, you thought of everything!"

"Probably not," he said, though her admiration warmed him. "Come look at the spring house. I'm surprised it's still standing. I expected the stream to overflow and take the wood with it."

Mary knelt beside the water. A small wooden box stretched across the stream. She lifted the lid. It was empty.

"The tray is in the cabin," Aaron said. "I drilled holes in it so water can flow through. Milk and butter will stay cold.

"How did you think of that?" Mary asked.

He shrugged again, a little embarrassed. "It was just floating around in my head with all the other ideas."

Mary put her arms around Aaron and kissed him. "I love

it. Let's go unpack."

They unloaded the wagon. Aaron brought wood in and started a fire for her. Mary hung a pot on the hook and added water and dried venison to stew.

The table and chairs they had transported in pieces came together quickly in Aaron's skilled hands.

Mary looked at Aaron. "Where are all your tools?"

Aaron grinned. "We passed them on the way here." He laughed at Mary's confusion.

"Get back in the wagon. I'll show you."

Aaron turned the wagon around and drove it back down the path, stopping at the curtain of hanging vines.

"Why are we stopping?" Mary asked.

Aaron grinned as he helped her down. Picking up a large stick, he moved the vines and revealed the cave.

"Oh!" Mary exclaimed. "How clever."

"Be careful," Aaron warned. "The vines are poison ivy. They will make you miserable, but they're perfect for hiding this place."

Inside, cool air breathed out of the darkness, carrying the scent of wet stone. Mary hesitated, not from fear, but from the strangeness of stepping into a place where only a few people had been.

"Look at the ground before you go any farther," Aaron said. "I sweep it every time I leave. No tracks means no animals inside."

He led her to the large room behind the waterfall. She looked around and stared, awestruck. "This is incredible."

Aaron lit a fire behind the stone wall, then a torch. "The tools are in the next room."

Mary followed Aaron up the tunnel. All of Aaron's tools

were dry and in perfect condition. Mary started picking up the smaller tools to carry back to the wagon. Aaron brought the heavier tools. Finally, the cave was empty, and they returned to the cabin.

Mary relit the flame under the stew while Aaron put the tools in the barn and tended the horses. By the time Aaron finished assembling the table and chairs, the sun was going down. They sat down to eat their first meal in the cabin.

"We are really here," Mary said, smiling.

Aaron nodded. "Hard to believe, isn't it?" He yawned. "I'm tired. It's been an eventful day."

The open doors let in enough evening light for Mary to clean the kitchen. Darkness had settled by the time they finally crawled under the covers of the oversized bed.

The next several days passed in steady labor. Aaron plowed and planted. He cut the clover to dry for the horses. Mary helped sow grains and plant the garden.

When the planting was done, Aaron hung the shelves he'd made. Mary quickly arranged her containers of salt and grains on them.

A rhythm settled over them. Mary made corn pone cakes for breakfast. Aaron cleared more land. Mary ground wheat and corn for bread. Lunch was often fried rabbit, raccoon, or whatever Aaron's traps provided, along with wild greens or leather britches, and fresh bread.

Every afternoon Mary wandered the woods and meadows learning the land and looking for wild food. Garlic and mustard greens were plentiful, along with wild onions, blueberries and blackberries. She even found cattails growing in a slow moving part of the stream.

By July, every day was spent picking vegetables to eat, dry, or store in the root cellar Aaron had dug into the side of a steep hill. One morning Mary served corn pones covered with a sweet blue syrup.

"This is good," Aaron said. "How did you make it?"

"It's just honey and crushed blueberries cooked together." Mary sighed. "All we need is some butter. Oh, how I miss butter and milk."

"You found honey?"

Mary smiled. "There are three hives nearby. I think the bees liked the clover flowers."

Aaron leaned back, thinking. "How would you like to go with me to the salt flats?"

"I'd like that," Mary said. "When?"

"Let's go tomorrow. We'll pack supplies on the draft horses. I've got plenty of sacks. We'll keep some salt here and take the rest to Norfolk. James will want some, and we can sell some to Edward."

"I'll get food ready and pack the panniers," Mary said.

Aaron stepped outside to prepare the farm for their absence. He packed one pannier with sacks, small spades, and hay for the horses. By evening, everything was ready for an early start.

CHAPTER 23

Appalachian Mountains, Virginia 1743

The sky was only beginning to turn pale when Mary smothered the hearth fire, pressed venison and a corn pone into Aaron's hand, and mounted her horse. Aaron passed her the reins to one of the draft horses, and he took the other. A gentle nudge to their horses, and they were on the trail.

Two nights later, they were camped at the foot of the ridge they would have to cross in the morning.

"This looks like hard work," Mary said, eyeing the trail that wound up the slope.

"It is," Aaron said. "It's slow going up because the trail is steep, and we'll have to walk the horses over part of it. The other side is slow, too, because it's steep and slick. But we'll manage. Red Wolf and I have done it before, so I know the easiest way up."

By the next evening, they had finally crossed the ridge and reached the base of the far side, aching from the long climb and descent.

Mary dropped onto a fallen log and gave a weak, breathless laugh.

"I have never been so tired in my entire life!" She handed him a strip of dried venison and some berries. "There are more corn pones in the bag, but I can't reach it. I'm too tired to move."

Aaron chuckled. "I'll get it."

He fed and watered the horses, while Mary stretched out on her furs. When he returned, she was already asleep, her face soft in the fading light. It wasn't even dark yet. Aaron smiled, settled against a log, and took the first watch.

At dawn, Mary gently touched Aaron's shoulder. "Sun's up. I have breakfast for you."

Aaron sat up, accepted the food, and ate while she handed him water. After eating, he crouched at the stream and splashed cold water on his face, gasping at the shock.

"Agh! That'll wake a man," he said. "All right. Let's load everything. We have a lot of sacks to fill."

They rode in silence until the salt flats came into view. Aaron halted in the trees and watched the clearing with patient, practiced caution. No movement. No voices. No danger. They were alone.

Mary took the sacks and a spade. "I'll fill the sacks. You keep watch."

She worked quickly and quietly. It took almost three hours to fill all the sacks. As she finished each one, Aaron tied it off and placed it in the panniers.

She had just filled the last sack when Aaron stiffened. He heard horses. Several horses were approaching from the south.

"Get on your horse and go to the woods," he said quietly, pointing to the north side of the clearing.

Mary obeyed without question, riding toward the trees and leading the two pack horses. Aaron stood beside his horse just as the riders came into the clearing. There were men and women in buckskins, all moving with the easy confidence of people who knew the land.

The group stopped. The leader raised his hand in greeting. "I am Oganasti of the Cherokee."

Aaron said in Iroquois, "I am Pale Bear, friend of the Nottoway and Seneca. It is my hope to be friend to the Cherokee." Aaron was having a little trouble with the language. It was almost Iroquois, but not quite, and he felt the gaps as he spoke.

Oganasti nodded. "I have heard of Pale Bear. I have heard that he is a friend to the Iroquois and that we have nothing to fear from him."

He dismounted, walked forward with a calm confidence, and extended his hand in greeting.

Aaron clasped his forearm. "I am happy to meet Oganasti of the Cherokee and count him as a friend." He motioned for Mary to come out of the woods.

"This is my wife, Dancing Rain, of the Nottoway," Aaron said. Mary smiled and nodded respectfully to Oganasti.

While Oganasti and Aaron talked, Mary helped the Cherokee women fill their containers with salt. The work went quickly. When they finished, the women lingered at the edge of the woods, gossiping and laughing softly. Mary listened, amused by their jokes, and grateful for the easy camaraderie.

At last the men were finished with their conversation.

Mary and Aaron headed east, and the Cherokee traveled south.

"What did you and Oganasti talk about?" Mary asked.

"Rumors, politics," Aaron said. "They hate the English but feel they must ally with them for trade. They hope the French will drive the British back across the water."

"So, nothing useful."

"No," he replied. "Not really."

"That's good," Mary said. "At least we know there isn't a major Indian war starting. The women were talking about the men. They think some of the men are lazy. They're worried about another smallpox outbreak. And they told me about some plants in the mountains that are edible. That part was useful."

A few days later, they were back at the cabin picking the ripe produce from the garden. Mary laid several cotton cloths in the sun and placed blueberries, blackberries, and beans on them to dry.

Aaron used every spare moment he could find to clear more land. By the end of the summer, he had cleared another two acres, plowed it, smoothed it, and planted winter wheat.

In early September, Aaron said, "We need to make a trip to Norfolk to take the salt. Do you think we have enough supplies to get us through the winter and spring until we can plant again?"

"I've been stretching the wheat with cattail pollen and roots," she said. "But even then, I don't think we planted enough corn, wheat and oats to last the whole winter and spring. You can hunt and keep us in meat, but we need more than meat to stay healthy. And I don't think we have enough hay and oats to keep the horses strong. As much as I want to stay here, I think we need to go to Norfolk at least November through March."

Aaron nodded. "I agree. We will harvest everything we have and leave at the last possible date, but before the snow starts. I will get more land cleared. Every inch of land cleared is an inch available for crops."

CHAPTER 24

It was late October. Everything had been cleared from the barn and house except the hay, mattress, and a few pieces of household pottery containing salt. The rest was stored safely in the caves. The hearths stood cold and swept clean. Their clothes, food, and grains were packed in the wagon along with the salt, hides and furs they planned to sell.

Eating dried venison and leftover corn pone, Aaron and Mary climbed into the wagon for the long trip to Norfolk.

"I hate leaving," Mary said, "but I cannot wait to see everyone again."

Aaron smiled. "I know. I feel the same."

A cold wind blew down from the north. Mary shivered.

"Oh my," she said. "I'll not be sorry to miss that cold wind." Even with her buckskins, she wore a wool coat and kept a blanket tucked over her lap.

The trip down the mountain was slow, but once they were in the piedmont and on better roads, Aaron pushed the pace whenever he could. The weather had turned unsettled, and Mary tired more easily now. Still, they stopped only long enough to rest and water the horses. Nearly two weeks later, they pulled their wagon into the barnyard of the tavern.

Gordon spotted them and ran over to help Aaron with the horses. Aaron helped Mary from the wagon, and as soon as her feet hit the ground, she ran to the kitchen door.

James was inside gathering an order for some men in the tavern when the back door opened, and Mary walked in. For a heartbeat, he simply stared, then crossed the room and wrapped her in a fierce hug.

"I was hoping that you two would be smart enough to come here for the winter," he said, pulling back.

His eyes dropped to her stomach. "What's this?"

"Your grandchild," Mary said. "He or she will be born before we go back to the farm."

Blair came over and embraced her. She patted her own stomach. "Our baby will come after you leave."

Mary beamed. "I'm so happy for you."

Outside, Aaron and Gordon carried in the extra food from the wagon. James joined them and pulled Aaron into a hug.

"I'm glad to see you," he said.

"And I you," Aaron said. "I put our grain harvest in the brewing room, but I'll likely use most of the oats for the horses. I had to leave my hay."

James waved a hand. "Don't worry about the horses. I have plenty of hay and grain. Those Fletcher boys are good workers, but I think they'll be leaving me in the spring. They're planning a trip to the Brunswick Courthouse after the new year to apply for land."

"Good for them," Aaron said. He handed James three sacks of salt. "We thought you could use some."

James laughed. "Aye. This more than makes up for any hay or grain your horses may use."

"Is there a room upstairs we could use?" Mary asked.

"Aye, there are several open. Pick whichever one you want," James said smiling. He remembered the order and took it out to the dining room.

The next day Aaron took the salt and pelts to Edward to sell. Edward handed him an accounting of his investment.

"You're becoming a rich man, Aaron."

Aaron laughed. "It's nothing I'm doing. You're the businessman."

They talked for a while, and Edward shared the latest news of the colony. When Aaron gave Megan a list of supplies, she scanned it and laughed.

"Mary must be planning to do a great deal of sewing," Megan said.

Aaron grinned. "She is. We have a baby coming in February."

Megan gasped softly. "That's wonderful! We'll get to see your son or daughter before you return."

On his way back to the tavern, Aaron saw Gordon stepping out the front door. Gordon waited for him.

"I'm going to the docks," he said. "A ship just came in. It's likely the last one for a few months. Very few souls dare to cross the north Atlantic Ocean in winter unless the courts are transporting them."

"I'll walk with you," Aaron said.

The wind off the water was sharp for an eastern Virginia November. The docks smelled of tar, salt, and wet rope. Gulls cried overhead and the ship's rigging creaked in the gusts. Many of the passengers shivered on the deck, their clothes thin and travel-worn. The first mate lined up those who could not pay their passage; they would be offered as indentured servants.

Gordon nodded toward two boys. "See those two lads? I think they're Angus Abernathy's boys."

"Abernathy?" Aaron asked. "Why would he put his boys on this boat? They would be needed on the farm."

When the boys reached the dock, Gordon approached them. "Are you Angus Abernathy's boys?"

"Yes, sir," the older one said. Anxiety flickered in their eyes.

Gordon waved Aaron over. "These are definitely Abernathy's boys."

Aaron crouched slightly to meet their gaze. "What are your names and where are your parents?"

"I am Bruce," the older boy said. "And he is Alan. Our parents died of the fever that swept through Scotland last summer. The Laird was going to place us with another family, but we decided to take ourselves to Virginia. We had no money, so we will work off our passage."

Aaron walked to the first mate and paid the boys' debt. Returning, he said, "Your passage is paid. You are safe and will have a good place to live and work. Come with us."

Bruce hesitated. "Sir?"

Aaron turned, "Yes?"

Bruce flushed. "What are we to call you, sir?"

Aaron smiled. "Forgive me. I should have introduced myself. I am Aaron McNeil, and this is Gordon McNeil of

Clan McNeil."

"McNeil?" Bruce asked. "Our clan?"

"Aye," Aaron said. "Gordon watches the docks and every passenger on the boats. We have helped several members of our clan."

Gordon looked at Bruce, "No, *he* has helped several members of the clan, including me and my wife. Aaron is the Laird's third son who went missing three years ago."

Bruce and Alan looked at Aaron in open awe.

"The Laird's son?" Bruce whispered. "The one they say is a frontiersman?"

Gordon smiled. "Aye."

"He doesn't look like a frontiersman," Alan murmured, glancing at Aaron's clean coat and polished boots.

"No," Gordon said, amused. "He's wearing what he calls his English clothes. When he puts on his buckskins to go into the wilderness, he looks the very part of a frontiersman. He's a good man. We're fortunate he was here for us all. Come on. Let's get you a bath and some food, in that order."

Gordon led the boys to the brewing room and showed them how to fill the tub. He handed them soap, towels and a change of clothes.

"Where did the clothes come from?" Alan asked, running a hand over the soft linen. He kept glancing about the room as if unused to being somewhere safe.

Gordon chuckled. "Aaron was about your size when he came over. He grew... a lot, but they kept his clothes in case other immigrants needed them."

In the kitchen, warm with the smell of stew and fresh bread, Aaron turned to Mary.

"Don't be mad," he said, "but I paid the passage for two boys on the boat. They're from my clan at home. Their parents died, and they chose indentured service rather than stay in Scotland."

Mary smiled. "Now, why would I be mad about that? I'd like to meet them."

Gordon brought Bruce and Alan into the kitchen. They were clean, with damp hair, and were wearing Aaron's old clothes. Bruce stood straight, trying to look older; Alan hovered a step behind him, taking everything in with wide, cautious eyes.

"You two look better," Aaron said. "Sit at the table and we will get you some food. Eat small and slow today. Let your stomach adjust to land and better fare."

When the boys were settled, Aaron said, "Mary, this is Bruce and Alan Abernathy. Boys, this is Mary, my wife."

They stood at once. "It's nice to meet you Mrs. McNeil."

"My, you two have excellent manners," Mary said warmly, "but please, call me Mary like everyone else does." She shot Aaron a mischievous look. "You may call him skunk man."

Aaron burst into laughter. Everyone stared, which only made him laugh harder.

"No, you may call me Aaron," he said to the boys. He looked at the others. "I had an encounter with a skunk in the mountains. The skunk won."

Understanding dawned across the room, followed by chuckles.

"What did you do?" Blair asked Mary. "How long did you make him stay outside?"

"A few days," Mary said. "A few baths helped him, but even boiling and washing his clothes in lye soap did not help them. They hung over bushes for almost two weeks! I hid his buckskins and would not let him put them on until he no longer smelled like that awful animal."

Bruce and Alan exchanged astonished glances. They were teasing the Laird's son! That would never have happened in Scotland. Aaron caught their expressions and laughed again.

Aaron asked, "How old are you lads?"

"I'm sixteen," Bruce said.

"I'm fourteen," Alan added.

"You're young enough to learn different ways," Aaron said. "In Virginia, I'm not a Laird's son. I am just Aaron, a hardworking man trying to make his way in this new land. We're all on equal footing here. You and I are equals, or we will be once your indenture is over. I have a chance to be better than I could have been in Scotland, and so do you. Work hard, and when the time comes, I will help you get land to start your own farms."

The door opened. Evan and Jamie Fletcher stepped in and stopped short.

"Bruce? Alan?" Jamie asked.

"Aye," Bruce said. "We just got off the boat."

Evan looked at Aaron. "Thank you, Aaron. They're our friends from back home." He turned to Bruce. "Your parents?"

"Died with fever during the summer," Bruce said quietly. "We decided to try Virginia over having to work for someone else in the clan."

"Smart," Evan said. "You chose rightly."

Bruce hesitated then looked at Aaron. "Sir, I mean Aaron, the Laird's wife died with the fever, too. I thought you'd want to know."

Aaron went still. A small, quiet ache crossed his face. "Thank you for telling me," he said softly. "I imagine Father is quite sad." For a moment he pictured his father alone in the great hall, the fire burning low. Whatever distance lay between them, the news still settled heavily in his chest.

He looked at Evan. "Evan, may I put these two in your hands to learn about Virginia and help around the tavern? You may as well tell them about the farm in the mountains. I'm going to let them help me up there for a year or so, until they are older and strong enough to make it on their own."

"Yes, sir. I'll teach them about helping here." Evan hesitated. "Aaron, are you planning to go hunting again this winter?"

"I hadn't decided yet. I was going to go see if Red Wolf wanted to go. Why?"

"I'd like to go with you," Evan said. "Jamie will stay here, but we want to get some land, and we were thinking it might be a fine thing to get our land in the mountains near you. It would be like starting a new clan. I need to scout the area, and it would be easy to do that from your farm."

At the words, *a new clan,* Bruce and Alan exchanged a look that was hopeful, almost disbelieving. The idea seemed to settle into them like warmth.

Mary said, "Aaron, I was wanting to go visit Red Wolf. If we do that soon, you can plan a hunting trip. I think we are going to need more buckskins." She widened her eyes and tilted her head meaningfully toward the Abernathy boys.

Aaron smiled. "Let's plan on going to the village tomorrow if the weather is good." He turned to Evan, "I think we can go hunting. I'll invite Red Wolf."

Evan and Jamie took Bruce and Alan out the back door. Aaron heard Alan ask, "Who's Red Wolf?" He chuckled when he heard Evan tell him, "You have no idea about this place."

The day was clear and warm for November. Bruce and Alan were eating at the kitchen table when Aaron and Mary came down the stairs dressed in buckskins. The boys froze, staring.

Alan whispered to Bruce, "He really is a frontiersman!"

Aaron grinned. "Morning lads. Has Evan put you to work?"

"We've milked the cows for Blair and gathered the eggs," Bruce said proudly.

"That's a fine start," Aaron said. "They will probably have you out cutting wood later today. We will be back tomorrow or the next day."

He and Mary ate a quick breakfast. Aaron hitched the horses to the wagon, and they started the trip to Red Wolf's village.

"Are you comfortable?" Aaron asked. "The journey will be a rough ride in places."

Mary shrugged. "Let's go slow and not bump and jostle. It should be fine."

By late afternoon, they reached the village. Red Wolf came out of the lodge to see what the commotion was, then broke into a smile and came to help Mary down from the wagon.

"Dancing Rain seems to have grown big around the middle," he said.

She laughed. "Yes. It is quite a change, is it not? But I am quite happy about the expansion in my stomach."

Red Wolf and Aaron clasped hands. "It is good to see you, Pale Bear."

"And you, Red Wolf. Mary wanted to visit, and I hoped to invite you on a hunt."

"I am happy to go hunting, Pale Bear. I will bring White Eagle with me."

Aaron blinked. "White Eagle is old enough to hunt? Red Wolf, your boys are growing up too fast!"

Red Wolf smiled. "Yes. I miss their little days. When did you want to go?"

Aaron pulled a sack of salt from his saddlebag and handed it to Red Wolf. "If we could stay the night, I'll return home tomorrow and be back in three days. Our travel is slow. Mary doesn't want too much jostling in the wagon."

"Dancing Rain is wise," Red Wolf said. "Most women avoid horseback or wagon travel when they carry a babe."

"She has," Aaron said. "But she wanted to see you and your family."

"She is already in the lodge with Bird Song," Red Wolf said. "You are welcome to stay with us tonight. Come. Let's set one of your traps for a rabbit."

Later, Aaron sat scraping the rabbit skin and smiled as he watched Mary talking and laughing with her uncle, her aunt, and White Eagle. Running Bear sat in a corner. Aaron realized Running Bear was sulking. The boy's shoulders were tight, and his eyes were sharp with resentment. Aaron thought that one day he would come to the village and Running Bear would be gone. He would be off with other restless young men looking for a fight.

That night, a cold wind curled around the lodge, but inside, the furs were warm and soft. Mary snuggled close.

"We need some of these on our bed before we spend a winter there," Mary said.

"I suppose there will be no more selling the pelts for a while," Aaron said, smiling. "That's all right. Those furs made me a wealthy man. I would rather have a warm wife."

"We need to make another mattress if those boys are going back with us. They can sleep in the loft." Mary yawned. "I'll think about that later." Aaron smiled as she drifted to sleep.

Three days later, Aaron and Evan rode into the Nottoway village. Evan tried not to stare, unsure if curiosity would be rude, but everything fascinated him.

White Eagle ran up to Aaron. "Pale Bear, are we staying in a cave?"

Aaron laughed. "We used to. I have a cabin now."

"Oh." White Eagle's face fell.

Aaron said, "But I suppose if you and Red Wolf want to spend a night there that would be up to your father."

White Eagle brightened. "I would at least like to see the cave."

"We can arrange that," Aaron said.

Red Wolf approached with his horse and a pack horse. "White Eagle where is your horse?"

White Eagle turned to point. The spot was empty.

"It was right there!" he exclaimed.

"If you want to hunt, you must always know where your horse and rifle are," Red Wolf said sternly, though his eyes gleamed with amusement.

"Where's my horse!" White Eagle shouted, sprinting behind the lodge.

Red Wolf chuckled. "His friends are pulling a prank, but it teaches a valuable lesson."

Aaron laughed as White Eagle's voice echoed between the lodges. "Where's my horse!"

One of the boys brought the horse to Red Wolf. White Eagle rounded the corner and stopped short. "You had my horse?"

"No, I did not," Red Wolf said calmly. "But it seems I do now. Let this be a lesson. You were lucky to get your horse back this time. The next time you may not be so lucky, and you will lose your supplies and have to walk."

White Eagle flushed. "I know," he muttered.

Red Wolf softened. "It was a prank. While we are gone, you may think of one to get back at your friends."

White Eagle's face lit up. "I will think of the best one yet."

He mounted his horse and rode beside Aaron, peppering him with questions. Red Wolf and Aaron answered them all until they left the main road. After that, the forest swallowed their voices, and they traveled in companionable silence.

CHAPTER 25

Appalachian Mountains, Virginia 1744

The cold had settled deep into the mountains. It was the kind of cold that made the air feel sharp in the lungs and left a crust of ice on every branch. Snow covered the ground, giving the horses' hooves a muffled crunch on the earth. Aaron's breath rose in pale clouds as he worked.

He knocked the snow and ice from his moccasins before going into the cabin. He was grateful for the extra fur lining Mary had sewn into them. Thinking of her warmed his chest, but guilt twisted in his stomach. She must be huge with the babe by now. He pictured her moving slowly around the kitchen, one hand pressed to her back, her belly rounded beneath her apron. He needed to get back.

"I am ready to go," Aaron said to Red Wolf. "If you wish to stay longer, you may use the cabin."

Red Wolf smiled. "I am ready as well. I think White Eagle would stay longer, but he will go with us."

Aaron smiled, glancing at Evan. "I know Evan is ready

to get home. You want to collect Jamie, get to Brunswick Courthouse, and file your claim."

Evan's grin widened. "You're right about that."

"Get Jake Webster to do the survey," Aaron said. "He did mine, so he knows the area."

Evan nodded. He had found the perfect property for him and Jamie. It was a rolling stretch of good soil with a creek that ran clear even in winter, and enough timber to build a home. Aaron was happy for him. He remembered that soft assurance, the knowing that you were home.

Aaron's packhorse carried a large stack of pelts, tightly bound and smelling faintly of winter and woodsmoke. Red Wolf's horses bore sacks of dried meat for his family and village. The panniers on the animals bulged with tools and sacks of salt. They all rode with a restless energy. Each man had a different reason urging him eastward, but all were eager to return.

Bundled warmly against the cold, they faced the rising sun and began the journey home.

Mary was kneading dough when the back door opened, and a gust of cold air swept in. She looked up, and there he was. He stood tall and strong, cheeks flushed from the cold, eyes warming at the sight of her. She held her back and walked slowly toward him.

Aaron crossed the room in three strides and bent to hug her, breathing in the familiar odors of flour and hearth smoke mixing with her own unique scent.

"I missed you," he said softly. "Are you well?"

Mary smiled up at him. "I missed you, too. I am well, and the babe is very active. If I counted correctly, we should be parents by this time next month."

A flicker of fear crossed his face before he could hide it. "I am nervous about the baby coming. I don't want you to hurt."

Mary touched his cheek. "Don't worry. I think my time will be like most Nottoway women, uncomfortable, but bearable and quick."

He nodded, but the worry didn't leave his eyes.

A week later, the Montgomery and McNeil families waved goodbye to Evan and Jamie. The young men had spent the money they received from Fletcher on supplies, tools, muskets, powder and shot. Aaron and James gave them seeds and provisions to last several months. Snowflakes drifted lazily as the brothers rode away, and Aaron felt a quiet pride watching Evan begin his own life.

Two weeks after that, Mary stopped kneading dough and pressed a hand to her back. A tightening rippled through her belly. When it passed, she resumed kneading, her breath steady. Twenty minutes later, another contraction came, slightly stronger. She smiled to herself. This baby was coming.

Aaron came out of the brewing room, pleased with the latest barrel of spirits. He looked up to see Red Wolf and Bird Song riding into the barnyard. Their horses snorted clouds into the air.

Aaron stopped and smiled. "Welcome. What brings you here?"

Red Wolf dismounted. "Bird Song says it is Dancing Rain's time, and she wanted to be with her. It is a woman's time and women support each other."

Relief washed over Aaron. "Mary will like that."

He opened the door and motioned for Bird Song to enter. Mary looked up in delight.

"Bird Song!" she said in Iroquois. "You have come! How did you know?"

Bird Song's eyes sparked. "Rain Flower is not the only one who can have a vision. I am here to help you give birth to your son. When did your pains start?"

"This morning," Mary replied.

Aaron blinked. "You've been in labor, and you didn't say anything? Should you not be in bed?"

Mary laughed softly. "The pains are mild and far apart. It has given me time to get everything ready in the bedroom."

Bird Song nodded approvingly. "It is good to work and be distracted as long as possible."

Red Wolf entered carrying a piece of shaped wood. Bird Song took it, placed the furs around it, and handed it to Mary.

"A cradleboard!" Mary looked at Red Wolf and Bird Song with tears glistening in her eyes. "Thank you. How did you know I wanted one?"

"Pale Bear asked how to make one," Red Wolf said. "I told him we would give you one as a gift."

Bird Song lifted a basket filled with cattail pods. "Do you have these?"

"I have a few. There are not many around here. I made the belt last summer from extra buckskin. Thank you for these. They will help keep the baby dry, too."

Mary sat down. She cut a pod open and began to remove the soft, fluffy inside. Bird Song joined her, their hands working in rhythm. Every few minutes, Mary paused, closed her eyes and breathed through a contraction.

"Is that a labor pain?" Aaron asked, hovering.

Mary nodded. "They are closer together now and a little more uncomfortable."

"Good," Bird Song said. "Keep working."

Mary laughed and went back to her chore.

The tavern filled with evening noise, clinking tankards, murmured conversation, and the smell of stew and bread. Molly and Blair worked quickly, glancing often at Mary. James dropped a tankard of ale, swore under his breath, and was told to stay behind the counter in the dining room.

As the sun was going down, Mary grabbed Bird Song's hand during a contraction.

"It is time to go to bed, Dancing Rain," Bird Song said. "Show me your room."

Aaron and Bird Song helped Mary up the back stairs and into the bed. Bird Song shooed the men out of the room and asked Aaron to bring warm water.

Bird Song surveyed the room. "You are well prepared, Dancing Rain. That is good."

When the tavern began to clear of patrons, Blair came into the room to sit with Mary.

"I would have come sooner," she said, "but tonight was busy, and James was no help. He is pacing and keeps dropping things."

Mary smiled weakly. "My mother died in childbirth. He is scared."

Blair's expression soften. "Oh. That explains it."

Bird Song checked Mary again. "It is almost time." She looked at Mary. "Send Blair to ask Pale Bear if he would like to come see his son born."

Blair hurried downstairs and returned with Aaron, whose face was pale but determined. He took Mary's hand; Blair held the other.

Bird Song spoke in Iroquois, her voice calm and steady. "Pull on their hands, bear down, and push."

Mary did. The room filled with the sounds of effort, Mary's breath, Aaron's encouragement, and Bird Song's low chant. After several pushes, the baby slid into Bird Song's hands.

She smiled. "Your son is a healthy babe."

Downstairs, the tavern fell silent for a heartbeat, then erupted into cheers when the baby's cries rang through the floorboards.

Blair helped Bird Song tie the cord and cut it. Mary placed the baby on her chest, guiding him to nurse. When the placenta delivered, Blair and Bird Song cleaned the bed and replaced the sheets. Mary put on the belt with the cattail fluff to collect the still-draining blood.

Aaron and Mary watched as Bird Song cleaned the baby, wrapped him in a blanket and handed him to Mary.

Mary took Bird Song's hand. "Thank you, Bird Song. I will always be grateful to you for coming."

Bird Song smiled warmly. "We are family. That is what we do. What will you name him?"

"James Neil McNeil," Mary said. "We will call him Jamie."

Aaron went to fetch James. When he entered, Aaron said, "Meet James Neil McNeil. We will call him Jamie."

James froze, stunned. Tears glistened in his eyes. "I have a grandson."

Aaron said softly, "He is named for the two men who saved my life, you and my father."

James sat heavily in the chair, and Mary handed him the baby.

He looked at Bird Song. "Thank you for helping Mary. I am forever grateful."

Red Wolf had slipped into the room, and he translated James' words. Bird Song smiled at James, then at Mary, her eyes shining with pride.

Later, Aaron sat beside the bed, watching Mary cradle their son, and felt something settle deep inside him, something calm and sure. He thought back on the last night in the castle, about the voyage across the ocean, about the fear and uncertainties, the learning, the joys and hardships he had experienced. A certainty rose in him as steady as the mountains around their cabin. He had forged a home in the wilderness, but now he was a father, and his way of seeing the world was different. Nothing in his life would ever be the same.

CHAPTER 26

Norfolk, Virginia 1744

A few days after Jamie was born, Aaron watched Gordon make his way to the docks. A ship had come in, its rigging creaking sharply in the cold wind blowing off the Elizabeth River. Aaron followed, already imagining the misery of crossing the Atlantic in winter. He imagined the cold damp that never left the bones. Only government transports would attempt such a voyage this time of year. No immigrant would willingly brave it.

They stood together as the passengers were herded out and lined up on the dock. Neither man recognized any of them. Aaron's gaze caught on a girl of about thirteen, trying to fold herself into nothing. She stood with her shoulders hunched and eyes down, as if hoping the boards beneath her might swallow her whole. A few men nearby snickered, making crude remarks about "getting that one."

Aaron didn't hesitate. He strode over to the first mate and said quietly, "I'll pay for the girl."

The money was in the man's hand before anyone else

knew what was happening. When the men on the dock realized she was walking away with Aaron and Gordon, they protested.

"You didn't give us a chance to bid on her!" one shouted.

Aaron turned. The look he gave the man was a cold, ferocious, unblinking anger that made him step back without another word.

When they were at the top of the hill, Aaron stopped. He crouched slightly so he wasn't towering over her.

"My name is Aaron McNeil," he said gently. "You have nothing to fear from me or anyone in my family. What is your name?"

"Christine O'Neal," she whispered, her Irish brogue trembling.

"O'Neal?" Aaron said, softening. "Well, we may have some kin way back." He studied her face, which was thin, pale, and too young for the haunted look in her eyes. "How old are you?"

"Thirteen, sir."

"Why were you being transported?" he asked.

Christine swallowed hard. "I went to work in one of the big houses in London. The mistress said she did not like Irish girls. She handed me over to the magistrate to be deported." Her voice cracked. "I worked hard, but she was so mean!"

Aaron took her hand. She flinched at first, then let him.

"That won't happen here." He nodded to Gordon. "This is Gordon. His wife Blair will help you get settled."

Aaron looked at Gordon. "She can sleep with Molly for now." He exhaled. "I guess I had better get another mattress made."

Gordon let out a short laugh, then stifled it when Aaron shot him a look.

Inside the tavern, Aaron led Christine to the kitchen. Molly and Blair looked up and exchanged a knowing glance, trying not to smile.

"Don't laugh," Aaron warned. "She's only thirteen and you know what those men on the docks wanted." He turned to Blair. "Will you help her bathe, eat, and get settled?"

Blair's expression softened. She stepped toward Christine with open warmth.

"Welcome to Virginia, Christine. Every one of us has been through what you have, and every one of us has Aaron to thank for our good fortune. He came over the same way, young and scared."

Christine blinked, startled, then looked at Aaron with new understanding. "Thank you, sir."

"You're welcome," Aaron said. "Now go with Blair. She'll take care of you."

When they left, he looked at Molly. "Where's Mary?"

Molly pointed upward.

Aaron climbed the stairs, pausing outside their room before entering. Mary sat in the chair nursing Jamie, the winter light falling softly across her face. She looked up immediately. She knew his silences too well.

"Just say it," she said. "What's wrong?"

Aaron sat on the bed, rubbing his hands together. "I bought another passage at the docks."

Mary laughed, shaking her head. "I'm not surprised. Is it another McNeil?"

"No. An O'Neal. Her name is Christine. She's only thirteen." His voice tightened. "The men on the docks were betting on who would get her. I just put the money in the first mate's hand and walked away with her. She's terrified. I don't know how she made the crossing without being harmed. Maybe because she looks younger than she is."

Mary's smile faded into something tender and fierce. "Where is she?"

"Blair's giving her a bath and a change of clothes. She'll be back soon to eat."

Mary lifted Jamie to her shoulder to burp him, her brow furrowing. "I want to go downstairs and make her welcome." She paused, thinking through the logistics.

"What?" Aaron asked.

"We need another mattress and blanket plus pillows for her and the boys. What does she have for clothes?"

"Just what she's wearing," Aaron said.

Mary sighed. "Then you'll need to take me to Edward's store. I need bolts of cloth, scissors, thread, and needles. She'll need boots, but maybe those can wait until next fall. I can make her moccasins for inside the cabin and for warm weather. Thank goodness we have the summer to get her a coat made." She continued. "Buy more corn, wheat, and oats. I can stretch them with cattails. Acorns make good flour, too."

That afternoon, Aaron took Mary to the general store. Megan looked at the growing pile of supplies. "Is this all?"

"Probably not," Mary said, "but I can't think of anything else."

Megan smiled knowingly as she held Jamie. "He took in another one, didn't he? These kids have no idea how fortunate they are. I talk to a lot of bond servants running errands. A lot are apprentices learning a trade, but some of them live miserable lives. Some don't survive their first year."

Mary nodded. "Aaron is a good man. And I'll admit that I'm grateful. It'll be good to have a girl to help with the chores the men don't have time for. Clearing the land and getting crops to grow is demanding."

"It is," Megan agreed. "But if anyone can make it work, it's you two."

Mary looked at the pile again. "Aaron can come back for all this with the wagon."

"I can come back for what?" Aaron said, then saw the mountain of supplies. "Oh. We'd better go if I want to get the wagon here and back before dark."

Bruce and Alan helped Aaron hitch the wagon, retrieve the supplies from the store, and unload them in a storage shed behind the tavern.

When Jamie was about three and a half weeks old, Aaron said, "Mary, would you come outside with me?"

Mary followed him into the yard. He had arranged the supplies in the wagon to create a bed with the mattresses, pillows, and soft furs from his hunting trip.

"Could you travel in this?"

Mary ran her hand over the soft furs, feeling the mattresses beneath them. "Oh, this is wonderful. Thank you, Aaron. Put my head up near you at the wagon seat and the crates with the chickens at the other end. I will walk a lot, but this will be a blessing when I can't."

Aaron stepped behind her and tickled Jamie under the chin. The baby, swaddled snugly in the cradle board, blinked up at him.

"I think he just smiled at me," Aaron said, astonished.

Mary laughed softly. "Of course he did. You're his father." She shook her head, amused. It would be another two weeks or more before Jamie could smile on purpose.

Two days later at sunrise, Aaron drove the wagon out of the tavern barnyard. Everyone waved goodbye. Mary settled down comfortably on the mattresses with Jamie. Christine rode beside Aaron while Bruce and Alan rode the two horses. A cow plodded behind the wagon, and chickens squawked indignantly at every jolt.

James stood with his arms folded, trying not to show how sad he was. Next winter, the tavern would feel emptier without them seeking shelter in Norfolk.

The journey was slow and maddening. They could only travel as fast as the cow could walk. Twice they had to stop, pull tarps over the wagon, and wait out a cold rainstorm. Afterward, they slogged through mud that sucked at the wagon wheels.

At last they reached the foot of the mountain. Mary walked the entire way up to lighten the load on the wagon. The draft horses strained only once, their breath streaming in the cold air.

When the cabin came into view, Mary nearly wept with relief. She was exhausted. Her recovery had been incomplete when they left Norfolk, and though she was healed now, the journey had drained her strength. She leaned back against the furs and smiled. She would get up in a minute.

Strong arms lifted her before she realized she had fallen asleep.

"Hold Jamie tight," Aaron whispered. He carried her into the house and laid her gently on the bed. "Sleep. The boys, Christine, and I will take care of everything."

Jamie's cry woke her. She turned her back to the kitchen and let him nurse. When he was satisfied, she rose. It was still light outside. Someone had stacked wood in the hearth, so she lit the fire. A bucket of water sat beside it.

Then she noticed the rest. The hinged hook was reinstalled. The cooking pot hung over the hearth. Sacks of flour, salt, sugar, cornmeal, beans, potatoes, dried apples, and a cured ham sat on the table. She had slept through all of it.

Christine came through the door carrying knives, spoons, ladles, and forks. She placed them carefully on the table.

"I didn't know where you wanted your things or what you wanted to cook for supper."

Mary smiled. "It's fine, Christine. I shouldn't have slept so long. Let's start some stew."

She showed Christine how to cook over an open hearth and how to make corn pone. While the stew simmered, Christine helped her fill jars with staples and place them on the shelf.

"I'll ask Aaron to hang that ham in the corner," Mary said. "We'll fry some for breakfast."

Aaron came in carrying a folded piece of canvas. "You're awake. Good. I can hang this."

He slid a large dowel through the fold of two canvas pieces and nailed the dowel to the wall. When he finished, the curtains opened and closed smoothly.

"Thank you, Aaron," Mary said. She turned to Christine. "You'll sleep on a mattress in the main room for now. We'll think of a way to give you some privacy."

It was dark when Aaron, Bruce, and Alan entered the cabin. Venison stew with potatoes simmered in the pot, and hot corn pones warmed on the hearth. Mary smiled when she heard their stomachs growling.

Aaron had the boys help him assemble the long bench he'd built in Norfolk. Now five could sit around the table. Mary and Christine filled five bowls with stew and set the corn pone in the center of the table.

"You all look exhausted," Mary said. "I'm sorry I fell asleep." She looked at Bruce and Alan, "Did you get your mattresses and clothes in the loft?"

"Yes, Ma'am."

"And the extra wool blankets?" she asked.

"Yes, Ma'am."

"Well, good," Mary said. "I declare you four finished for the day. Rest, talk, walk, sleep, whatever, but enough work has been done. I'll clean up the kitchen."

When the meal was finished, Mary cleaned the dishes and the cooking pot. Every bit of stew and corn pone had been eaten. She would need to cook larger meals from now on.

Aaron, Alan, and Bruce stepped outside for a moment, then returned. Bruce and Alan climbed the ladder, and it sounded like they collapsed straight onto their mattresses.

Aaron grinned up at the ceiling. "They worked hard today."

"I'll cook bigger meals," Mary said. "They're still growing. I need to finish their leggings and skirts. Bruce looks like he's about to outgrow what he's wearing."

"It's good we brought all those hides," Aaron said. He picked Jamie up and held him. "He's growing fast, too. Look how well he holds his head up."

Jamie smiled at Aaron and reached his tiny fist toward Aaron's face. Aaron smiled. "You're a smart one, little man. We'll have you hunting and fishing in no time."

Mary took Christine to the outhouse. When they returned, Mary helped her position her mattress on the floor.

"You choose where you'd like to sleep in this room," Mary said. "We'll make you some privacy."

Christine nodded. She was too tired to care. She lay down fully clothed, pulled the blanket over herself, and fell asleep instantly.

Mary went into her bedroom. Jamie slept in his cradle. Aaron was already asleep. She lay down beside him and drifted off within minutes.

CHAPTER 27

The days settled into a steady rhythm. Breakfast was at first light, then the men went out to plant the crops and clear more land. Mary and Christine cooked, gathered wild greens and onions, and collected pollen from the cattails. Mary noticed a patch of wild strawberries near the creek. They were still small and green, but promising.

They began setting regular days for washing, cleaning, sewing, and mending. Mary planted apple seeds in a box to see if they would take root. The quiet work of the homestead filled the hours, and the land slowly began to look lived in.

One afternoon as Mary stepped out with a bucket of dishwater, she heard a call from the trees. "Ho the house!"

Her heart lurched. She handed Jamie to Christine and whispered, "Go to the barn. Find Aaron."

Mary stepped into the yard, forcing her breathing to steady. The woods felt too still, as if holding their breath with her. When two riders emerged, she exhaled with relief. It was Evan and Jamie.

"Hello!" she called, smiling.

Aaron came running from the barn. He stopped short when he saw who it was. His shoulders dropped with the same relief Mary felt. Everyone gathered on the porch, catching up on news and progress.

Mary rose after a few minutes. "Christine and I will get supper. You men keep talking. Evan, you and Jamie are welcome to stay the night."

She was glad she had planned a fresh rabbit stew. The meat had simmered all day, rich and fragrant. She added onions and potatoes. In a bowl she placed wild greens with chopped onions and poured hot ham fat over them to wilt. Fresh bread and corn pones went into a basket and set on the table.

There were just enough wooden plates and utensils for the seven to eat. Seating was another matter.

"If you boys will bring in the bench from the back porch, I'll move my chair to Aaron's side," Mary said. It worked well enough, and everyone squeezed in together.

Evan told them he and Jamie had built a cabin on one side of the boundary and a barn on the other. They had just improved both farms. Clearing the land was slow, but they had an acre planted in corn and hoped to have two more cleared soon for oats and clover, maybe wheat this fall.

"James said we could winter in Norfolk like you did last year," Evan said. "We may have to."

Aaron nodded. "Our harvest will be before yours. If you come help us, we will help you with yours. If you wish, you can winter here with us, but we won't force you. A warm bed in Norfolk beats a straw mattress in an attic any day.

"Thank you," Evan said. "We'll accept your offer of help and start here with your harvest."

In midsummer, Aaron said, "I want to take a few days and get salt. Will you be alright staying here if I leave Alan?"

"Yes," Mary said. "Take Evan and Jamie. All of you together can bring back a good load."

The next morning, Aaron and Bruce rode off, with plans to stop by Evan and Jamie's farm. Mary watched them disappear into the trees, a faint unease settling into her chest. The woods felt too quiet again.

When they were gone, Mary asked Christine, "Can you fire a weapon?"

"No," she answered.

Mary handed her a pistol and showed her the basics. Christine listened carefully, her face pale but determined. Mary loaded the gun and handed it to her.

"Keep this in the pocket of your skirt," Mary said. "Let's hope we don't need them. If trouble comes, they won't expect two women to have guns. Also, be ready for wolves, mountain lions, or wild pigs."

She told Alan to carry his rifle at all times.

"We only get one shot," Mary said. "We have to make it count."

Mary also strapped a hunting knife and sheath to her leg.

"Oh, one more thing," Mary said. "If Indians come into the yard, under no circumstances are you to aim a weapon at them. Let me handle it. Most of them are our friends."

Alan and Christine stared at her.

"Your friends?" Alan asked. "Back in Scotland, all we heard about were the heathens who want to kill everyone."

"Whoever said that wanted an audience," Mary said. "It's not true. Now, let's get back to work."

Nearly a week passed. Mary began scanning the tree line hoping to see the men returning.

"They should be home any day now," Mary said at breakfast. "I'll rest easier when they are back."

Alan went to the field to hoe the corn. Christine went to milk the cow. Mary cleaned the kitchen, moving in and out of the house. Jamie was asleep in his crib.

She was stepping outside with her dishwater when a voice said, "Well, hello, Ma'am."

Mary spun around. A man stood beside the house, holding the reins to his horse. He was filthy, and she could smell him even from several feet away. Something in the way he watched her made the hairs on her neck rise.

"Can I help you?" Mary asked, keeping her voice steady and slowly setting down the bucket of water.

"I reckon so," he said with a leering smile. "Looks like you're all alone. Need some company?"

"No. You can keep traveling."

The man took a step closer.

Mary took a step back. "I said keep traveling. Do not come any closer."

Christine came out of the barn with the bucket of milk, saw the man advancing toward Mary, and ran to get Alan.

"Well, I feel the need to get closer," the man said. "I haven't been around a woman in months. Seems like you could get closer so we could talk."

When he lunged, Mary's hand was already in her pocket. She drew the pistol and fired. The shot echoed through the clearing. The man looked stunned then crumpled to the ground.

Alan and Christine came running. Jamie started crying.

"Make sure he's dead. I must get Jamie," Mary said calmly, though her hands were trembling.

When she returned, Alan said, "He's dead."

"Check his clothes for money or valuables," Mary said. "Then check his saddle bags. And take care of the horse. If he didn't take care of his horse any better than he did himself, it may need extra attention."

Alan unsaddled and tethered the horse, then pointed to the man. "What do we do with him?"

"Drag him to the stream," Mary said. "Make sure he floats down far enough to go over the falls. By the time anyone finds him he will be unrecognizable."

Alan dragged the body away. Christine stayed beside Mary, watching her closely.

"I need to reload the pistol," Mary said and walked back into the cabin. She picked up the shot and powder, but her hands were shaking so badly, she couldn't pour the powder into the barrel. Christine calmly took the gun, loaded it and placed it on the table.

"Are you alright?" she asked softly. "Did he hurt you?"

"No. It just happened so fast. I've never killed a person before. It feels... different. Not like a deer or rabbit."

"You were brave," Christine said. "You protected yourself."

Alan walked back into the cabin. "He should be going over the falls about now." He sat at the table with Mary and Christine. No one spoke. Mary noticed Alan's hands trembling slightly, probably from the trauma and exertion of having to dispose of a dead body.

Jamie let out a loud protest at being ignored. Christine took him from the cradleboard and handed him to Mary. The act of holding Jamie and giving him attention grounded her and brought her back to the needs of the moment.

Finally, Alan said, "I need to hoe the corn, but I feel a greater need to stay up here with you in case he wasn't alone."

Mary smiled and put her hand on his. "After what's happened, I think that's wise." She looked around the cabin. "Let's make Christine a room."

Christine chose a spot along the south wall. Alan fetched small trees that had been cut before the men left and fashioned a frame. They stretched canvas across the poles to form two walls with the cabin wall making the third. Christine moved her mattress inside, and Alan built a small table for her hairbrush or a candle.

Mary smiled. "What do you think, Christine?"

Christine touched the canvas gently. "It's perfect. Thank you."

Just before supper, Alan said, "I need to fetch the hoe I dropped in the cornfield. I'll be right back." He ran to the field and returned quickly.

"You must have run," Mary said, laughing.

They ate and secured the cabin. Alan pulled his mattress downstairs, sleeping in the middle of the room with a loaded musket beside him.

The next morning, they worked together; breakfast, cleaning, milking, gathering eggs. Mary kept glancing toward the woods, listening for hoofbeats.

"How many hoes are in the barn?" Mary asked.

"Three or four," Alan said.

"Then let's all three go and hoe corn until it gets hot."

They worked for three hours, the sun rising warm and bright. Every rustle in the woods made Christine jump; every shadow made Mary's hand drift toward her pocket and the pistol hidden there.

"That's enough," Mary said at last. "Let's go back to the house. Jamie needs a new diaper. He stinks.

Alan put the hoes in the barn and they returned to the cabin. Mary fixed a noon meal with vegetables and dried venison.

"I like this squash," Alan said. "There are so many different foods here."

"I like it too," Mary said and explained to Alan and Christine about the three sisters — corn, beans, and squash — and how they grew best together.

After lunch, Mary took Alan and Christine to the edge of the woods to gather wild mustard greens for supper. The air was warm, the leaves whispering gently overhead, but Mary found herself glancing toward the deeper shadows of the woods. The trauma from the day before was still too fresh and left her with a heavy sense of unease.

On the way back to the cabin, they heard horses coming up the path. All three froze. Mary's heart thudded painfully.

"Run!" Mary whispered.

They hurried to the house, slipped inside, barred the

door, and watched from the window. A moment later, familiar figures emerged from the trees. It was Aaron and the others. Relief washed over Mary so suddenly her knees nearly buckled.

Aaron had been eager to get home. As he rode up the trail, he expected to see Mary or Christine in the yard. Instead, the clearing was empty, and a strange horse stood tethered in the barnyard. A cold dread gripped him.

He raised a hand, signaling the men behind him to stop. He pointed toward the unfamiliar horse, his jaw tightening. He dismounted quietly and started toward the cabin.

The door opened. "Aaron!" Mary called out, her voice breaking with emotion.

Relief surged through him. Mary ran into his arms, Jamie strapped to her back. He held them both tightly, breathing in the familiar scent of her hair and the warmth of the child.

"What happened?" he asked, seeing Christine and Alan step onto the porch. Alan held a musket. Mary was shaking, tears streaking her cheeks.

"What happened?" he asked again, softer this time.

Christine spoke. "Yesterday. Mary was in the yard. Alan was in the cornfield. I came out of the barn with the milk and saw a man in the yard talking to her. Something felt wrong, so I ran to get Alan. We both came running. The man lunged for Mary, and she shot him. After you left, she made sure we all carried loaded weapons. She and I hid pistols in our pockets. After that, we did every chore together. We didn't separate."

Aaron nodded, absorbing every word. He pulled Mary close again.

"You were brave," he murmured. "You protected yourself and our son. I'm proud of you. Did he hurt you?"

Mary shook her head no.

"Where is the body?" Aaron asked.

"He went down the waterfall," Alan said quietly.

"That's good enough." Aaron turned to Evan and Jamie. "You're welcome to stay for supper and the night. It's been a long day."

They accepted and helped tend the horses.

"Mary, is there enough to feed us all?" he asked.

Mary nodded. "I expected you back. There's plenty of stew over the fire, bread, wild greens and onions, stewed squash, and tomatoes."

Aaron held Jamie while Mary and Christine finished preparing supper. Alan stayed close, helping where he could. He and Christine were the youngest of the group and still carried the strain of the past days. All three of them had been traumatized by the incident. Their movements were careful; their eyes looked tired. Aaron could see how deeply the experience had affected them.

He felt a pang of guilt. This farm was not on any commonly used trail. Why had a lone white man been out here at all? Seneca or Cherokee hunters he could understand, but not this.

Supper was lively on the men's side of the table. Evan, Bruce, and Jamie told stories of the long journey to the salt flats and how they now had enough salt to last the winter. But Mary, Christine and Alan were quiet, exhaustion softening their faces. The fear that had kept them alert and vigilant was slowly ebbing, leaving only fatigue. Christine's new canvas-walled room and Alan's mattress on the downstairs floor were silent proof of how closely they had stayed together.

That night Aaron held Mary close.

"You're a brave woman," he said. "You did what you had to do. But it's alright to feel troubled about taking a life. I know. The first time I killed anyone was those two men at the salt flats. It took days before I could accept that I'd done the only thing I could to survive."

Mary rested her head against his chest, letting his steady heartbeat calm her.

"You'll come to peace with it," he whispered.

The next morning Mary and Christine fixed breakfast while Alan went to the barn to milk the cow and get the eggs. Normally Christine did the milking, but Aaron suspected it would be some time before the three of them slipped back into their old routines. Fear had a way of rearranging habits.

Evan and Jamie Fletcher left for their farm. Aaron, Bruce, and Alan took hoes and went to the corn field. Aaron stopped short when he saw how much had been hoed.

"How did you get all this done?" Aaron asked.

"After our little incident, the three of us stayed together," Alan said. "All three of us hoed this field yesterday morning."

"You're a wise lad," Aaron said. "Thank you for being here for Mary and Christine."

Alan's face tightened. "I'm sorry, Aaron. I'm sorry I

wasn't at the cabin to stop that man. I'm sorry Mary had to be the one to kill him. It has shaken her badly."

Aaron put a hand on Alan's shoulder. "No one could have predicted it. You dropped the hoe and ran to help. That's what any man in your position would do. Christine didn't freeze; she ran for you. Just seeing you two coming gave Mary strength. You didn't hide. That's bravery, Alan. You proved yourself to be a brave lad, and I'm grateful. It's over now and time to move on to the next crisis, which today happens to be weeds choking our corn crop."

Alan managed a small smile at Aaron's humor. "Aye, that is a crisis. Thank you for understanding, Aaron."

"You're welcome," Aaron said. "I've lived through everything you have since leaving Scotland. I understand more than you think.

A few days later, Mary walked around the shelves, evaluating their stores. They had dried vegetables, corn, wheat, oats, potatoes, turnips, pumpkins, butternut squash, dried blueberries and blackberries, and honey.

"What are you thinking?" Aaron asked, lifting Jamie from the cradleboard.

"I'm thinking Jamie is too big for the cradleboard. My back is killing me. But I don't know how to work and watch him, too." Mary sighed. "Also, I'm trying to gauge if we can winter here, especially if Evan and Jamie come."

"I can make a chair he can sit in and play," Aaron said. "As for winter, I think we'll be fine. Evan and Jamie will bring supplies if they choose to come. I saw their farm. They'll have a good harvest for the land they cleared."

"Next year I want to grow cotton," Mary said. "I don't have sheep for wool or flax for linen. Cotton is my pick."

"Cotton seeds it is," Aaron said. "Mary, I want to make a trip to Norfolk. Not a long one with a wagon, but a short one on horseback. I can take James a sack of salt, check with Edward about my investment, get news of the colony, and see if I can get the supplies for a still."

"When are you going?" Mary asked.

"After the harvest. I'll ask Evan if one of them wants to go," he said. "If not, I'll go alone. I don't want to leave you here with just Alan and Christine again."

"Will you be back for Christmas?"

"Yes."

"See if Edward has some sort of toy for Jamie. Bring back some linen or cotton cloth. And if you decide to buy any more passages, be prepared to add a room onto this cabin," she said with a grin.

Aaron laughed. "I'll try to not bring home any more waifs."

Mary kissed him. "Whoever you bring, make sure you have supplies for mattresses and extra clothes."

When the harvest was finished, Aaron started the trip to Norfolk. Bruce was left in charge of the farm and the tasks Aaron had laid out before leaving. The cabin felt strangely quiet without him, though Mary tried to keep the day moving as usual.

Shortly after lunch, Jamie Fletcher rode up the path. He found Mary near the cabin.

"I'm to shelter here until Evan gets back," he said.

"That's fine, Jamie," Mary said warmly. "You can sleep in the loft with Bruce and Alan. They're out clearing land, I think."

Jamie nodded and headed off to find his friends, leaving

Mary standing in the doorway, the breeze stirring her hair.

For the first time in several weeks, the yard felt peaceful. The shadows in the woods no longer seemed to hold threats. Inside, Christine played with baby Jamie, making him laugh. Outside the sound of axes rang through the trees. Life was returning to normal, and Mary was grateful for that.

Chapter 28

Norfolk, Virginia 1744

Evan and Aaron rode into the yard behind the tavern. Gordon spotted them and came over to take the horses.

"What brings you two back to Norfolk?" he asked. "Is everything all right?"

"All is well," Aaron said. "I just need some supplies and news."

Evan followed Gordon to the barn while Aaron stepped into the kitchen. James looked up, startled.

"Aaron! We weren't expecting you. Is everything all right?"

"All is fine, James. I'm making a quick trip for supplies and information."

"What sort of information?" James asked.

"Tell me about the colony," Aaron said. "Which way are the settlers going?" He wanted all the information he could get to prevent another traveler appearing at the farm with dangerous intent.

James filled him in on the newest arrivals pushing farther west, though he knew of no one besides him and

Evan in their area of the mountains. He caught Aaron up on Norfolk gossip and the latest happenings.

Blair came in carrying her baby.

Aaron smiled. "What have we here?"

"Aaron, meet Maggie McNeil," Blair said proudly.

"She's a fine-looking child," Aaron said.

"How old is Jamie now?" Blair asked.

Aaron grinned. "Seven months and running his mama ragged. He's too old for a cradleboard, too little to walk, and everything goes into his mouth. Christine has been a lifesaver for Mary."

Blair laid Maggie in a cradle and went to help Molly.

James leaned closer. "Aaron, word is that James Stuart has amassed quite an army in Italy. He has followers in Scotland and some in England. French sailors passing through say they expect him to cross the Channel next year. I thought you'd want to know."

"Aye, I do. Thank you, James." Aaron's face softened. "There's not a thing I can do for my kin except pray they stay safe."

After eating, Aaron said, "I brought you some salt. I'll fetch it." He returned with the panniers from his horse and handed James the sack.

"Thank you, Aaron. With all the newcomers, salt is dear at the general store. Edward gives me a discount, but it's still high."

Aaron grinned. "I have one sack for Edward, too. I'll go see him now. Maybe I can trade the salt for some cotton seeds."

"Cotton? Let me guess, Mary wants cotton," James said, laughing.

Aaron laughed. "That's right." He headed for the door.

"I'll be back."

Aaron left the general store after a long conversation with Edward and Megan. Edward had even more information on the Jacobites and their plans. He wished his father and Duncan were in Virginia.

The street started to make its slight slope to the docks. Aaron saw Gordon leaving the tavern. Beyond Gordon, he saw the masts of a ship lowering its sails as it docked. Aaron decided to follow him.

They stood watching the passengers.

"Recognize anyone?" Aaron asked.

"No, but if someone was a child when we left home, I might not know 'em now," Gordon said.

Passengers were claimed one by one until only a young boy and two small children remained. No one stepped forward for them.

Aaron went to the boy. "How old are you?"

"Ten, sir," he said.

"Where are your parents?" Aaron asked.

"They caught the fever on the ship and died, sir."

The younger two were fighting tears. Aaron's jaw tightened. "Come with me."

The first mate stepped forward. "Sir, their passage?"

"What about it?" Aaron asked coldly.

"You haven't paid for their passage."

Aaron glared at the man. "If you had treated your passengers better, you wouldn't be dropping three orphans off in a strange land. Do you want to take responsibility for them?"

"No."

"I didn't think so." Aaron turned to the boy. "Bring your

brother and sister."

Gordon helped the three children up the street. Once they were away from the docks, Aaron knelt so he was eye level with them.

"My name is Aaron. You are safe, and you will be taken care of. Now, what are your names?"

"I'm Edward McDowell," the oldest boy said. "This is Charles, he's eight. And this is Heather, she's five."

"Well, Edward, Charles, and Heather," Aaron said gently, "you're part of my family now. Let's get you some food."

Aaron led the three children through the tavern and into the kitchen. He turned to Gordon.

"Can you help the boys bathe? Edward is carrying a bag. They may have a change of clothes."

"Aye, I'll take care of the fellas," Gordon said.

Heather started to cry, wanting to go with her brothers.

"Let her go with you," Aaron said. "Her brothers can bathe her."

James approached. "Aaron, there were children at the docks?"

"Orphans," Aaron said quietly. "Their parents died on the ship. No one wanted three children." He sighed, feeling overwhelmed with his decision. "How do I get them home?"

"Get another wagon," James said. "Smaller this time. One your horse can pull or the two horses you and Evan have."

Aaron nodded. "I need to talk with Evan."

Two days later, Aaron and Evan sat on the seat of

another small wagon. The back was cushioned with straw mattresses, pillows and several blankets. Sacks of flour, sugar, tea, coffee, and cornmeal lined one side of the wagon. Powder, shot, and a basket of kitchen utensils filled a corner. Aaron tucked the children under blankets in the back, protected by a canvas cover.

At night they sat around the fire while Aaron asked the children about their lives. He learned their family had been ostracized by the other McDowells for refusing to openly support restoring James Stuart to the throne.

"We are Presbyterians," Edward said. "Da didn't think anyone should fight over religion. He said God wouldn't want that."

"Your father was a wise man," Aaron said softly.

Aaron drove the wagon up the path to the house and stopped at the front door. Relief washed over him at the sight of home, but he dreaded telling Mary what he had done.

Mary stepped out of the cabin with Jamie on her hip and gave Aaron a puzzled look.

"You have another wagon?"

Before Aaron could answer, three small heads popped up from behind the sacks of staples.

Mary's eyes widened. "The docks?"

"Orphans," he said quietly. He climbed down and took Jamie from her arms. "What else was I to do?"

Mary's expression softened. "You could do no less."

She walked around the wagon to the children. "Hello. My name is Mary, and this is where you are going to live. What are your names?"

"Edward McDowell, Ma'am."

"Charles McDowell, Ma'am."

"I'm Heather," the little girl whispered.

"Well, Edward, Charles, and Heather," Mary said gently. "Would you like to come inside?"

Edward helped his brother and sister climb down. Mary held out her hand for Heather, and the little girl took it. Mary led Heather by the hand and gestured for the boys to follow.

"You can come with me," she said. "Are you hungry?"

Inside, Mary set warm bread with butter and cups of milk in front of the children. She sat with them at the table.

"I'm so sorry your parents died," she said softly. "I know how that feels. My mother died when I was about Charles's age. It's all right if you are sad, but I want you to know that in our family you are safe and you will be loved. I'm very glad Aaron brought you home to us."

Aaron stood nearby with Jamie who was squirming and reaching for Heather.

"Heather," Aaron said, "this is Jamie. He seems to want to be your friend. Would you like to hold him?"

Heather nodded, and Aaron placed Jamie on her lap. Jamie leaned back against Heather and smiled.

Mary laughed. "Well, Heather, I do believe Jamie already loves you."

Jamie then reached for Charles. Charles took him, and Jamie relaxed again.

Mary smiled. "Charles, it looks like you have Jamie's approval, too."

When Jamie reached for Edward, the boy grinned and settled him on his lap.

Mary smiled. "Well, Jamie has just declared you three

to be his brothers and sister. Will you consider being his family?"

All three nodded.

"Thank you," Mary said. "Now, Heather, you can sleep with Christine in her little room." She pointed to the older girl. "Edward and Charles, you'll sleep in the loft with Bruce and Alan," Mary pointed to the steps going up.

Evan stepped into the cabin. "Aaron, I've unhitched the horses. Jamie and I need to get back to our farm."

Aaron shook Evan's hand. "Thank you for going with me. The trip took an unexpected turn, and I was grateful to have your help."

"Any time," Evan said. Jamie gathered his things from the loft and the two left.

Christine helped Heather settle into their room. Alan and Bruce took Charles and Edward to the loft. At supper, two adults, three teenagers, three children, and one baby crowded around the table. Christine, Alan and Bruce kept up a lively conversation, drawing the McDowell children in. Aaron and Mary watched, content.

"So, you're not mad?" Aaron asked.

"Never," Mary said. "I would never be angry over saving a child's life. I'm glad you brought them."

Aaron looked toward the table.

Mary noticed. "What are you thinking about?"

"I need to figure out how to make this table bigger," he said.

Mary burst out laughing.

On Christmas morning, Mary and Aaron rose early. Mary placed Jamie on the mattress between Heather and

Christine. Aaron milked the cow and gathered the eggs. Mary fried the rest of the ham, made corn pones, and cooked eggs. She set the table with butter, blueberry syrup, and a pitcher of milk.

When everything was ready, Aaron and Mary began calling out in a loud voice. "Get up! Time to get up! It's Christmas!"

The boys came down from the loft, and the girls emerged with Jamie. They were rubbing their eyes and yawning until they saw the table.

"Let's gather in a circle," Aaron said. "We'll give thanks for this day and our blessings."

After the prayer, Mary showed the children how to split the corn pone, butter it and drizzle syrup. Their delighted exclamations filled the room.

Aaron said, "I've done the milking, tended the horses, and gathered the eggs. No more work today until the evening milking. It's Christmas."

The children cheered.

Christine helped Mary tidy the table and hearth. Mary checked the turkey Aaron had shot the day before. It was still roasting.

When everything was in order, Aaron said, "Everybody sit back at the table for a moment."

The children settled into their places. Aaron went into the bedroom and returned with a stack of bundles wrapped in cloth and tied with string.

He handed one to each child. The children looked at him with expressions of curiosity and excitement.

"All right," Aaron said, "Open your Christmas present."

String flew into the air. Cloth wrappings piled in the center of the table, and then... silence.

"Is something wrong?" Mary asked.

Bruce shook his head. "No. I've never received anything like this for Christmas. It's perfect. Thank you." He held a set of buckskins and a hunting knife.

Alan had the same. "Thank you," he said.

Edward also received a set of buckskins and a hunting knife. "Thank you," he said.

Charles held buckskins and a sling shot. "Thank you. I always wanted a sling shot."

Christine received a new dress and a hairbrush. "Oh... thank you," she whispered.

Heather hugged her new dress and a soft, stuffed doll. "Thank you," she said.

Jamie grinned and banged his new blocks together. Everyone laughed.

"Go try on your new clothes!" Mary said. "I want to see if they fit."

The boys scrambled to the loft, and Christine took Heather to their room. Soon they all returned and proudly showed off their clothes.

Aaron stepped out of the bedroom with another package.

"Children," he said, "today is Mary's birthday." He handed it to her. "Happy Birthday."

Mary opened it and gasped softly. The package held a hairbrush, hair pins, and colored ribbons. "Oh, Aaron. This is lovely. Thank you."

Aaron smiled, pleased she liked it.

Christine and Heather stared at the ribbons.

"We will use these on special occasions," Mary said. "Like today!"

She tied ribbons in the girls' hair to match their dresses, then tied back her own long hair with another.

"Now, aren't we beautiful?"

"Yes, we are!" the girls chimed. Mary and Aaron laughed.

Outside, a cold wind swept across the mountains, carrying snow. Inside, the cabin glowed warm with firelight and laughter as the family played games and shared their Christmas meal.

CHAPTER 29

Rome 1745

John McNeil straightened his wig, checked the shine on his shoes, smoothed his stockings, and adjusted his cravat until it lay perfectly. He smiled at his reflection. A new year had begun, and he felt certain the time was near when he would return to Scotland in triumph at the side of James Stuart, the rightful king of England.

The hallway outside his chamber was crowded with men moving toward the ballroom of the manor that now served as the court of James III. John entered the room and began bowing, greeting, and exchanging polite words with the courtiers. But his eyes kept drifting to the far end of the room. There, surrounding James III and Prince Charles were Cameron, MacDonald, MacDonnell, and Stewart. They formed a tight circle, a circle John could not enter. His jaw tightened. These men only had to step into the room, and they were considered indispensable.

He had spent two years cultivating influence, flattering the right people, and maneuvering himself into the prince's notice. He had clawed his way from the lower ranks to a position of trust. Yet unease gnawed at him. His status had been purchased with promises. He was not Laird. He couldn't control the clan's men or money. Still, he'd promised the full support of the McNeil Clan and a generous financial contribution. He had written to Neil demanding the money, but no reply had come.

The lack of power infuriated him. His father's silence was humiliating. When he returned to London as part of the victorious court, he would see to it that Neil was deposed as Laird. John would take his rightful place.

A movement from the far end of the room brought John from his musings. Prince Charles had left his circle and was walking toward him.

"John," Charles said. "I would speak with you."

John bowed deeply. "I am at your service."

Charles smiled. "Those men around my father are old and of their generation. I am building my future court, and I would like for you to be part of it."

John's chest swelled. "I would be honored to support you when you take the throne after your father."

Charles lowered his voice. "I have received word from Scotland. Support among the clans is strong, and they have raised money for an army. I intend to take the Scots who are here and join those at home. I would have you come with us."

John would have preferred to stay in Rome, but he forced a smile. "Your confidence honors me. When do we leave?"

"As soon as the weather warms," Charles said. "We will sail to Scotland. I thought we might land at the Hebrides. You have a home there, do you not?"

"Aye," John said. "On the Isle of Skye, but I would advise landing on the mainland and marching east to Inverness or south to Glasgow."

"Can I count on your support for food for the troops?" Charles asked, ignoring John's advice.

"Of course," John said smoothly. "I will write my father and tell him what we require."

"Excellent," Charles said, and moved on.

Isle of Skye 1745

A messenger arrived at the castle with a letter from John. Neil broke the seal, already bracing himself.

Dear Father, I hope this letter finds you well. I will be coming to Scotland in a few months with Prince Charles to start the campaign to restore James III to the throne. We will land the ships in the Hebrides in the summer. I have promised Prince Charles that we will donate food to the army. We will need sheep, pigs, wheat, turnips, potatoes, and barrels of ale. I expect you to have them ready when we arrive. John

Neil swore loudly.

"What does he want now?" Duncan asked.

"Our souls," Neil said sarcastically. "He wants us to feed Prince Charles's army, but they are not going to buy from us. We are going to donate it."

Duncan's eyes widened then hardened. "We could not feed a whole army even if they paid, but to strip us of food before the next harvest is madness!"

"It is June," Neil said. "We may have time to prepare. Come. I want to show you something."

He led Duncan to his chamber. A large bookcase covered one wall. Neil pressed a hidden latch, and the bookcase swung inward, revealing a narrow doorway. He lit a torch from the hearth.

"Follow me."

They descended a stone stairway to a vast underground room.

"I don't know what our ancestors intended for this place," Neil said, "but I found it by accident. We can store grain and root crops in here. When the army has gone, we can return the food to the people."

"I wonder...," Duncan said as he began testing stones along the wall. A faint click sounded, and a door opened into a narrow passage leading to the sea.

"They were smuggling," Neil said. "This is perfect."

Duncan nodded. "I'll start moving food. Hopefully we have enough time." Duncan looked at the large landing on a stairway near the hidden room. "We can have the men put the root crops and grain there, then you and I can move it. If they don't know where it is, they can't tell John."

"Good idea," Neil said. "What about the livestock?"

Duncan smiled. "I know just the place. John never explored much. There is a meadow at the far northern edge of McNeil property on the mainland. It is hidden by a forest. We can drive the best animals there and leave some of the boys to guard them."

"Very well," Neil said. "You're in charge, but keep an exact accounting of what every farmer contributes."

Duncan and several men started collecting surplus

food. He told the farmers the truth, that an army was coming and would take what they had if they didn't set some aside. Duncan weighed every sack, counted every potato and turnip, and had the men load everything in longboats and row it to the castle. The food was placed in the open chamber, and every night Duncan and Neil moved it into the hidden room.

The best livestock was driven to the secret meadow. Only the smallest, thinnest and least productive animals remained.

By mid-July, everything was done. The tenants had a month's supply of food in their homes. All that remained was to wait.

A week later, word spread across the northwest portion of Scotland that Bonnie Prince Charlie had landed on the Isle of Eriskay.

"That's just a day's sail across the sea," Duncan said. "I would have thought they would have landed on the eastern side of the country."

"I cannot guess their minds," Neil said. "I only hate they are so close."

On the last day of July, the watchmen in the towers called down, "Ship coming."

A small merchant vessel eased into the wharf. John stepped off, his wig powdered, his coat immaculate, his expression sharp with purpose. He strode up the path to the castle and found Neil in his study.

"John! What a surprise," Neil said, rising.

"I wrote you that I was coming," John said sharply. "Do you have what I need?"

"You wrote?" Neil asked mildly. "I never received a

letter stating your plans. What was it you needed?"

John's eyes flashed. "I have come to Scotland with Prince Charles and his army. I promised to help feed his men."

Neil folded his arms. "You cannot take my tenants' food. We had a bad harvest last year. They barely have enough to get them to the next one, which is still weeks away. Charles will have to find his food elsewhere."

"Don't you dare embarrass me before the next monarch," John snarled. "I will get what I need, starting with your storerooms."

"John!" Neil called after him. "Do not do this!"

But John was already storming out. He and the soldiers with him ransacked the castle kitchens and storage sheds. They rode to every farm in the clan, taking food and livestock. At each home, families pleaded with him not to take what little they had.

John ignored them all.

By the time he had loaded everything on his ship, the haul was pitiful. Thin grain, meager vegetables, scrawny livestock. It was nothing like the bounty John had promised.

Staring at the wagons, John's face darkened. This was not enough. Not nearly enough. Charles would know he had lied. Charles would never let him in his inner council now.

John clenched his fists, fury burning through him. He was ruined. His father, Duncan, and the whole clan had ruined him. But deep down, was the question he would never ask. Had he ruined himself?

CHAPTER 30

Appalachian Mountains, Virginia 1745

Aaron stood on a small rise, hands on his hips, looking out over the farm. He was pleased. They had cleared enough land to plant ten acres of grain, rotating crops of corn, wheat, and oats through the seasons. He and the boys would start the oat harvest soon. Behind the barn sat two small granaries, their floors tight and cool, built from the hard gray mountain rock they hauled out of the fields as they cleared them.

Three acres were planted in potatoes, turnips, okra, beans, yellow squash, green speckled squash, tomatoes, sweet potatoes, and pumpkins. On the southern slope, a dozen young apple trees stretched their small branches to the sky. Mary had coaxed them from seeds and faithfully tended them, though they wouldn't bear for another year or two. Wild blueberry bushes sat transplanted in the sun near the cabin. By next year they would be heavy with fruit. The harvest this year would be good. They had been blessed.

Laughter drifted across the yard. Aaron turned to see

Jamie playing with Heather and Charles. Not a day went by that he did not thank God for his blessings, especially the children. From Bruce down to Jamie, each one was dear to him. And Mary was to have another baby in October. His heart swelled at the thought.

A faint crunch of footsteps pulled him from his thoughts. Aaron lifted his rifle to his shoulder and waited. When the figures broke through the trees, he lowered his gun and grinned.

Hiawachi walked into the clearing.

Aaron strode forward and clasped his hand. "It is good to see you, Hiawachi."

"And you as well, Pale Bear," Hiawachi said.

Heather and Charles stood frozen, wide eyed. They had never seen a Seneca warrior before.

"It seems your family has grown," Hiawachi said, glancing at the cluster of children.

Aaron laughed softly. "You could say that." His expression darkened. "The ships come to Virginia. Sometimes children are on them. I have six here that I rescued from the docks. It is a sad thing, Hiawachi. The greed of some captains who starve the passengers then sell them as servants to whomever can pay the fare. Many die on the voyage before they ever reach land."

"You speak truth," Hiawachi said. "The greed of some of the white men will never be filled. We came to hunt. Game grows scarce in our lands. We have to travel farther when our meat grows low."

"You are welcome to hunt here," Aaron said. "My children scare the game away from here, but it should be plentiful over by the western mountain."

Mary stepped out of the cabin, wiping her hands on her

apron. When she saw the visitors, she approached with a warm smile.

"Hiawachi," Aaron said, "this is my wife, Dancing Rain of the Nottoway."

Mary smiled and nodded.

"It is good to see the wife of Pale Bear looking happy," Hiawachi said with a respectful nod. Then he turned back to Aaron. "We will hunt maybe five, maybe seven days."

"Take what you need for your people," Aaron said. "There is plenty."

Hiawachi motioned to his men, and they slipped silently back into the trees toward the west.

Aaron and Mary turned to see the yard full of staring children.

"Have you all finished your chores?" Mary asked.

Charles tugged at Aaron's sleeve. "Were those real Indians?"

"Yes," Aaron answered. "Those were Seneca. Our friends."

"What were you saying?" Charles asked. "I didn't understand it."

"I spoke in their language," Aaron said. "They do not speak English."

"How did you learn it?" Christine asked.

"Mary taught me," Aaron said, smiling. He leaned into her and whispered, "Get ready for it."

"Will you teach me?" Christine asked.

"Me too!" echoed through the group.

Mary laughed. "Alright. Finish your chores. Evenings and spare time will be for learning. Reading, writing, arithmetic, and Iroquois."

"What's ear-o-qwa?" Charles asked slowly.

"Iroquois is the language the Seneca speak," Mary said. "It is the language of my mother's people as well."

Sunday afternoons and evenings after supper became the learning hours. Short lessons began in reading, writing, and arithmetic. Lessons in the Iroquois tongue filled the cabin with new sounds and laughter.

In early October, Evan and Jamie Fletcher arrived to help harvest the corn. When their own fields were bare, the McNeils returned the favor, working side by side at the Fletcher farm. Evan and Jamie planned to winter there this year.

Mary was walking slowly these days, one hand pressed to her lower back. She was ready for this baby to get here so she could work again without the constant ache. Christine was helping her with the washing when she suddenly froze, staring past Mary.

Mary turned and smiled. Red Wolf and Bird Song were dismounting.

Mary hurried to them and embraced them both. "What brings you to our farm? I hope you're going hunting."

"Red Wolf is hunting," Bird Song said. "I am here to help you birth your daughter."

Mary blinked. "How did you know I was having a babe?"

Bird Song's eyes sparkled. "I just knew. I always listen to the dreams and visions." Bird Song looked around the yard. "You have done well here. And so many children. You have been fortunate."

Mary lowered her voice. "Aaron brings the lost ones and orphans from the docks."

"Pale Bear is a good man," Bird Song said.

Aaron came around the barn and broke into a grin.

"Red Wolf! Bird Song!" He clasped Red Wolf's hands. "What brings you to the mountains?" He looked at Bird Song. "Ah, I should have known. You have visions like Rain Flower."

Bird Song smiled. "I wanted to see your daughter."

"It's a girl?" Aaron asked, delighted. He looked at Mary. "Looks like you get your wish. Lily McNeil will be in the family before long."

"Lily?" Red Wolf asked.

Mary smiled. "I let him name Jamie. He is letting me name Lily, in respect to my Nottoway family."

"That is a good name," Bird Song said. "Have you had any pains yet?"

"No," Mary said. Just then her stomach tightened. "Well... maybe." Mary looked at Bird Song. "Did you bring labor with you too?"

Bird Song laughed. "No. Tomorrow is Lily's birthday. It had to happen soon."

Mary's contractions grew stronger as the day progressed. She and Aaron fed the family, while Red Wolf and Bird Song helped the children with their Iroquois lessons.

Christine slipped close and whispered, "Are you going to have the baby?"

Mary nodded.

"Do you want me to take Heather to the loft tonight?"

"That might be best," Mary said. "Thank you."

Her labor moved quickly. Shortly after midnight, Lily McNeil slid into Bird Song's waiting hands. Just like Jamie before her, she had Mary's dark hair and Aaron's blue eyes.

The morning sun lightened the cabin, washing away the strain of the night and bringing the joy of introducing Lily to the family. The children stood around the bed gazing at the tiny baby. They admired her for a moment, then as children do, they ran outside to do chores and play.

Christine fixed the breakfast and cleaned the dishes and pans. Then she came to sit with Mary and Bird Song.

"Would you like to hold her?" Mary asked.

Christine nodded, and Mary placed Lily in her arms. The baby blinked up at her then fell asleep.

"She feels safe with you," Mary said softly. "That is good."

Christine smiled, her voice hushed and full of emotion. "She's beautiful. I love her already."

"I think she loves you too," Mary said.

Christine looked at Bird Song and in Iroquois said, "Thank you for helping Dancing Rain."

Bird Song smiled. "You are welcome."

CHAPTER 31

Scottish Hebrides 1745

An early autumn chill swept around Neil McNeil's castle, long before the season should have turned. After John had taken every bit of food from the clan, Neil sent scouts to be certain his eldest son was truly gone. When word came that John had sailed with the stolen stores, Neil ordered the livestock back. Then he and Duncan moved the remaining food from its hiding place in the stairwell.

That evening, Duncan returned to every farmer the food he had stored. When the tenants learned that John had also taken the Laird's supplies, they quietly brought a portion of their food to Neil. He was grateful and humbled by their generosity.

By September, as the harvest began, Neil felt confident the clan would survive the winter. A rider brought news: the Scots had defeated the English at Edinburgh and were driving them south.

Neil thanked the man, then turned to Duncan. "It's too early to tell. But I cannot imagine a small Scottish army defeating the mighty British army."

"I heard that some of the Lairds forced their tenants to fight in the Scots army," Duncan said.

"Aye," Neil said. "I've heard that, too. Did any of our tenants ask to go to fight?"

"No, and they're grateful you have not forced them. Do you think John will come back when this is over?"

"I don't know," Neil said quietly. "But it would be better if he did not return."

"I agree," Duncan said. "And I think every tenant would agree with you as well."

Neil gave him a sideways look. "When are you going to marry and give me grandchildren?"

Duncan laughed. "Whenever I can find a lass who'll have me!"

"You will," Neil said. "Be patient, you will find the right one." He clapped Duncan on the shoulder. "Let's have some supper."

CHAPTER 32

Norfolk, Virginia 1745

In early November Aaron traveled to Norfolk with a load of salt and furs. Before going to Edward's, he stopped to see James.

Aaron walked into the tavern's kitchen with a sack of salt in his hand. James looked up and smiled.

"Aaron! Good to see you. Bringing salt and furs to trade?"

"Aye," Aaron replied and handed James the sack. "I brought furs to trade. I need slates and pencils for learning and Christmas presents for the children." Aaron grinned, "And you have a new granddaughter, Lily."

James blinked then grinned. "Another one? A girl?" He shook his head. "I would love to see her."

"Why don't you come back with me," Aaron said. "Come for a visit. I'll bring you back whenever you want."

James declined but said, "Maybe next year. I'm getting old. I need to see my grandchildren." He hesitated then added, "I'm going to talk with Edward about this place. It's turning a profit, but if he'd buy my half, I would come to the mountains." He gave Aaron a pointed look. "But don't tell Mary that. I'd hate to raise her hopes and disappoint her."

"I'll let you surprise her," Aaron said.

When Aaron returned to the farm, his pack horses carried flour, sugar, vanilla, chocolate, cornmeal, slates, paper, ink, quills, and bolts of material. He purposely arrived late enough that the children were asleep. Quietly, he carried the Christmas presents inside and hid them in the bedroom, then brought in the supplies. After tending the horses, Aaron crawled under the covers of his oversized bed.

"Thank you for making it so warm," he whispered.

"Don't put your cold feet on me!" Mary hissed back.

Aaron chuckled softly. "I missed you."

"I missed you, too."

Chapter 33

Scottish Hebrides 1746

Neil McNeil sat in his study, reading the month-old newspaper Fletcher had brought.

"This is over a month old," he muttered. He looked at Duncan. "Charles beat the English at Falkirk. He must be annoyed. They had been so close to London, and Falkirk is in Scotland."

Worry had become Neil's constant companion. He worried about John, and he worried about what would happen to the clan if the English won.

In late April Neil was at Fletcher's, sampling the latest whiskey, when a rider galloped up to the house.

"Sir," the man called. "The English won. The cause is lost."

"Details, man!" Neil snapped.

"It was a massacre, sir. Almost every Scotsman at Culloden Moor died or was taken. The prisoners are on ships. Some are to be executed in London." The rider swallowed, taking a deep breath. "The English are taking the lands of any clan that supported Prince Charles. Any lairds found to have aided him will be imprisoned or transported."

"Are the McNeils on the list?" Neil asked.

"Aye. That's why I came. To tell you. The English will be coming here sometime in the future to take your castle and land."

"Why?" Neil asked sharply. "We did not fight the English."

"You are listed as a supporter," the man said. "You provided food and money."

Neil closed his eyes briefly. "Damn." He exhaled. "Thank you. Do you need food for yourself or your horse?"

"Aye. I would be grateful."

Fletcher took the man to the kitchens and sent a groomsman to tend the horse. When he returned to the brewing room, his face was pale.

"What do we do?" Fletcher asked.

Neil was staring at the road. He straightened, resolve settling over him, and turned to Fletcher.

"We go to Virginia. We sail to London and look for those ships Ian used. I want everything of value taken. I will not leave a single coin or tool for the British to seize. Bring your brewing equipment." Neil started toward the door then turned back. "Start packing. We are going to write our own story. The English will not write it for us."

Neil strode quickly into the castle. "Duncan!" he called.

The staff froze. The Laird never yelled.

Duncan rushed from the study. "Father! Is everything all right?"

"Back in the study," Neil ordered as he climbed the stairs.

Once inside, Neil closed the door. "A rider brought the news. Charles lost the war. All is lost. It was a massacre at Culloden Moor near Inverness. I do not know what happened to John. But because he took our food, we are on the list of supporters. The English are coming to take our land and disperse the clan."

Duncan stared at him, stunned.

"I need you to call a meeting of all the men," Neil continued. "They must know. It's still morning. We'll meet at Fletcher's at four. It's central to the tenants. Be sure to let Fletcher know his property will be filled with men this afternoon."

Duncan blinked, momentarily still in shock, then he nodded and bolted from the room. He ordered men to row him to the shore. Once on the mainland, he sent messages to all the tenants. The Laird would speak at four o'clock at Fletcher's.

Neil summoned Morgan, his butler in charge of the household.

"Morgan, I need the entire house staff, groundsmen, guardsmen and any clan living on the island assembled. All of them. I have an announcement, and I only want to make it once. We have a lot to do. Have them gathered in the great hall at one."

The butler blinked, but bowed. "Yes, sir."

At one o'clock, Neil was sorting his valuables when Morgan knocked.

"Sir, everyone is waiting for you."

Neil nodded and followed him to the great hall. He stood on the lower stairs and looked out across the familiar faces, his relatives, and the people who had served his family for generations.

"I want to begin by saying you have all been loyal clansmen and servants of this house," Neil said. "You come from a long line of faithful McNeils, and I cherish that legacy."

He drew a breath. "Charles lost the war. James Stuart will not take the throne. The last battle was at Culloden Moor, and it was a slaughter. Any Scot who survived was taken prisoner. Because John took our food, our name is on the list of supporters. The English plan to take this castle and land and disperse our clan."

Gasps and murmurs rippled through the hall.

"I am going to take Duncan and Fletcher, and we are going to Virginia," Neil continued. "I tell you this so you may choose whether to stay or leave McNeil land. I will help you in any way I can. If you stay and things go poorly, get to London and find a ship to Norfolk, Virginia. You may have to be indentured, but it will be a short time compared to what life may become here."

Tears glistened on many faces.

"That is all," Neil said quietly. "Tell Morgan your decision."

Neil turned to the butler. "Find Cameron McNeil. He was not in here, and I need to speak with him."

"Yes, sir."

Neil started to walk away then turned back. "Can you find some men to take me to Fletcher's?"

"Yes, sir."

Neil paused. "What is your decision Morgan?"

"I will go to Virginia, sir. I cannot bear the thought of Englishmen living in our homes."

Neil nodded. "Good. We will go together. Find Cameron."

That afternoon, Neil repeated the speech to the rest of the clan. The same shock, fear, and grief washed over them.

When the men were dispersed, Neil turned to Fletcher. "Are you packing?"

"Aye. Where do we load what we're taking?" Fletcher asked.

"I'm looking for Cameron. He commands our largest ship. I'll tell you once I speak with him."

Neil found Cameron waiting for him in the great hall. "Cameron! Come with me."

In the study, Neil explained everything.

"Cameron, I want the *Bonnie Lass* loaded with every valuable we own, food, and as many of our people as she can safely carry. Outfit the other ship and appoint a captain to take anyone who cannot fit on the *Bonnie Lass* to London to get on a ship to Virginia. I want everything and everyone gone within one week. Can it be done?"

"Aye," Cameron said. "We'll be working long hours, but it can be done."

"Good," Neil said. He studied Cameron. "You have been wanting to make that passage, haven't you?"

"Aye, but it would have been better to make it in March. We will be going across the ocean at the time for those big storms."

"We have no choice," Neil said. "We will start and end every day with prayer for safe passage." He shook his head. "Why could those Jacobites not leave things alone?

Now we all suffer."

The next days passed in a blur. The clan worked with grim determination. Sadness at leaving their legacy mingled with the fierce resolve to leave nothing for the English. Everything that could be moved was loaded onto the ships or carried away. Slowly the McNeil land emptied.

It took two weeks, but Neil McNeil finally stood on the deck of the renamed *Mermaid's Legend* and watched his ancestral land grow distant. The castle was empty. Anything he could not take had been offered to clan members who were not going to Virginia. Wagons creaked away to family in other parts of Scotland or Ireland. No one had chosen to stay. The livestock was sold. Every vegetable and grain that could be wedged into the ship was taken.

Fletcher's manor house stood empty. Every tenant house was deserted. There was nothing left for the English.

Years later, Neil would hear from a Scotsman who lived in the nearby hamlet that the English had arrived only two weeks after the McNeils had sailed. The man said the English were furious to find the land stipped bare. Not an animal, chicken, vegetable, wagon or stick of furniture remained.

In London, Neil and Cameron looked for either of the two ships owned by Edward Montgomery. They found the *Virginia Spirit* moored nearby. After speaking with Captain Ivers, a plan was made. The *Virginia Spirit*, like the *Mermaid's Legend*, was primarily a cargo vessel, but a few of the members of the clan were able to board. The rest found passage on three more ships leaving for Norfolk. Neil paid every fare. No one would be indentured.

The *Virginia Spirit* and *Mermaid's Legend* left London a few days before the other ships. Neil hoped to reach Norfolk in time to help his people settle and find their way in Virginia.

During the voyage, Neil often battled anger, guilt, and melancholy. He was angry that John's ambition had forced the clan to flee Scotland. He felt guilty that his inability to rein in his eldest son had cost his people their homeland and legacy. All of it weighed heavily on him, leaving him with long, quiet hours of sadness.

Fletcher and Duncan recognized the burden Neil carried and did their best to reassure him that the people bound for Virginia would one day be grateful for this turn of events.

The gentle rocking of the ship, the vastness of the ocean, and the long days of reflection slowly began to work on him. Neil found himself letting go of the past, little by little. And he turned his thoughts toward the future. Soon he would see Aaron again.

Nine weeks after setting sail from London, the *Virginia Spirit* and *Mermaid's Legend* sailed into Norfolk. Neil, Duncan, and Fletcher stood at the rail and smiled. Somewhere in the middle of the ocean, they had stopped thinking of themselves as Scotsmen and started thinking of themselves as Virginians.

They were ready for the adventure.

Look for *Claiming the Frontier*, book 2 of the McNeil

Legacy. Neil, Fletcher, and Duncan McNeil adjust to the New World and reunite with Aaron. Aaron's family grows, and the land around him fills with farms and his clansmen. The McNeils weave their new lives around the politics of the colony including the French and Indian War. Life on the frontier is hard and sometimes perilous, but also rewarding.

ALSO BY A. K. GENTRY

<u>Whitlow Series</u>
An Awkward Inheritance, Book 1
An Unlikely Partnership, Book 2
An Unforeseen Danger, Book 3

The Perfect Loophole

<u>Forewarned Series</u>
Unprepared, Book 1
Second Chances, Book 2
Taking a Chance, Book 3 Coming Soon in 2026

ABOUT THE AUTHOR

A. K. Gentry grew up in rural North Carolina, USA. She has lived in small towns and rural areas all her life and loves bringing the small town values of faith and family to her writing.

Gentry is a retired registered nurse. She is married and has two daughters, one son-in-law, and two grand-daughters.